AF589152

A Literary Dog for Every Day of the Year

For Barley, who loves socks, and
Eppie, who was a Very Good Girl.

First published in Great Britain in 2026
by Cassell, an imprint of
Octopus Publishing Group Ltd
Carmelite House
50 Victoria Embankment
London EC4Y 0DZ
www.octopusbooks.co.uk

An Hachette UK Company
www.hachette.co.uk

The authorized representative in the EEA
is Hachette Ireland, 8 Castlecourt Centre,
Dublin 15, D15 XTP3, Ireland
(email: info@hbgi.ie)

Distributed in the US by
Hachette Book Group
1290 Avenue of the Americas,
4th and 5th Floors
New York, NY 10104

Distributed in Canada by
Canadian Manda Group
664 Annette St., Toronto,
Ontario, Canada M6S 2C8

ISBN 978-1-7884-0681-9
eISBN 978-1-7884-0684-0

A CIP catalogue record for this book is
available from the British Library.

Printed and bound in Great Britain.

10 9 8 7 6 5 4 3 2 1

Publisher: Lucy Pessell
Senior Editor: Katie Button
Assistant Editor: Samina Rahman
Designer: Isobel Platt
Typesetter: Karina Wong
Production Controller: Sarah Parry

This FSC® label means that materials
used for the product have been
responsibly sourced.

A Literary Dog for Every Day of the Year

Mischievous mutts
and faithful friends –
literature's waggiest tales

Tara Richardson

CASSELL

CONTENTS

INTRODUCTION

From Lord Byron's beloved Boatswain to Philip Pullman's cockapoos, dogs and writers seem to belong together. The Brontë sisters walked their dogs across the wild and blustery moors; John Steinbeck took his poodle Charley on a cross-country road trip in the 1960s. And as valuable as they are in terms of companionship, dogs can occasionally make shrewd editors. In this book, we'll meet more than one pooch who has seen fit to devour part of a manuscript, obliging the author to try again, no doubt improving on the original.

When they're not busy keeping writers company (or eating their homework), dogs also appear in many works of literature, whether they take on the role of central figures or add delight and intrigue as background characters. Over the course of this year, we'll meet crafty canines, princely pooches and even the occasional wolf. From the earliest of literary dogs, including Chaucer's medieval hounds and some Shakespearean pups, to the most ultra-modern sci-fi dogs, au fait with space travel and technology, the pages that follow contain 12 months' worth of daily dogs, sure to keep tails wagging all year round.

JANUARY

With the festive season firmly in the rear-view mirror and the winter months seeming to stretch out far ahead, January can be a cold, gloomy month – the perfect time, really, to turn to the glorious combined comforts of books and dogs.

Snuggle up under a blanket and read about a sled dog in the wilds of Alaska (12 January), or escape to the muggy warmth of the Indian jungle (18 January). This month's dogs are a clever bunch: they converse about society, debate philosophy with cats, run money-making schemes and even write letters. Most of all, though, they are loyal, from Greyfriars Bobby (14 January) waiting at his master's grave, to Argos (15 January) waiting for Odysseus to return after twenty years at war.

1 January

American author J D Salinger was born on this day in 1919. Although he is best known for the razor-sharp cynicism of his 1951 novel *The Catcher in the Rye,* Salinger also had a silly side. Today's dog is his pet Herman, who apparently could write almost as well as his master. The letter quoted below, in Herman's voice, was addressed to Jigger, the canine companion of a woman Salinger had met while on a cruise to Cuba in the 1940s.

Dear Jigger

How are you feeling I am feeling fine. Wile big shot is upstairs shaving his ridikilous face I am going to write you a letter jigger. He don't even know I can tipe, I can tipe better then he can and could write better storys if I felt like it, the trouble is I aint got the time.

I seen your mother when she was up to my house. Pretty tall and skiny but not too bad if you like that tipe. Old big shot hasnt been the same since he met her and she left on that plane, he jerks my leesh all the time and in general acts like a big jerk. I hope I see you soon jigger because I heard you was very attractive. I heard you wasnt no female but I was never one for splitting hairs on a little detail like that, besides my eyes aint too hot.

2 January

Today is Science Fiction Day. It falls on 2 January to mark the birthday of sci-fi legend Isaac Asimov, but today's dog was created by another big hitter of the science-fiction world, Philip K Dick. Boris is the canine narrator of Dick's short story 'Roog' (the first piece of work he sold). In the tale, Boris is alarmed by the creatures that regularly steal the food he has watched his master and neighbours carefully storing in containers outside their homes.

> The Roogs came toward the metal can, and one of them took the lid from it.
>
> 'Roog! Roog!' Boris cried, huddled against the bottom of the porch steps. His body shook with horror. The Roogs were lifting up the big metal can, turning it on its side. The contents poured out onto the ground, and the Roogs scooped the sacks of bulging, splitting paper together, catching at the orange peels and fragments, the bits of toast and egg shell.

3 January

J R R Tolkien, author of *The Lord of the Rings* and *The Hobbit,* was born on this day in 1892. Today's dog is Huan the Hound of Valinor, who appears in Tolkien's *The Silmarillion.* Huan is a powerful, loyal and fearless wolfhound, who has been gifted with the ability to understand speech – and to speak just three times in his lifetime. He fights wolves, helps Lúthien escape captivity and defeats Sauron in wolf form. Surely the very definition of a Good Boy.

> [N]othing could escape the sight and scent of Huan, nor could any enchantment stay him, and he slept not, neither by night nor day.

4 January

Poet and playwright T S Eliot died on this day in 1965. He is more commonly associated with felines, thanks to his much-loved *Old Possum's Book of Practical Cats,* but the collection does include a brief musing on the nature of canines:

> Now Dogs pretend they like to fight;
> They often bark, more seldom bite;
> But yet a Dog is, on the whole,
> What you would call a simple soul.

5 JANUARY

> When your children are teenagers, it's important to have a dog so that someone in the house is happy to see you.
>
> – Nora Ephron, *I Feel Bad About My Neck*

6 JANUARY

Although Arthur Conan Doyle never explicitly revealed the birthday of his iconic creation Sherlock Holmes, many fans choose today, 6 January, to mark the occasion. In Holmes's honour, today's dog is Toby, whom the famed detective borrows from one Mr Sherman in *The Sign of the Four*, in order to make use of his scent-tracking abilities. Watson, perhaps a little disgruntled at not being Holmes's only companion on this case, is not particularly complimentary in his description of Toby.

> Toby proved to be an ugly, long-haired, lop-eared creature, half spaniel and half lurcher, brown-and-white in colour, with a very clumsy waddling gait.

7 JANUARY

Naturalist and writer Gerald Durrell was born on this day in 1925. Today's dog is Roger, his constant companion in Durrell's much-loved book *My Family and Other Animals.*

I would suggest to Roger that perhaps it wasn't worth going out today. He would wag his stump in hasty denial, and his nose would butt at my hand. No, I would say, I really didn't think we ought to go out. It looked as though it was going to rain, and I would peer up into the clear, burnished sky with a worried expression. Roger, ears cocked, would peer into the sky too, and then look at me imploringly. Anyway, I would go on, if it didn't look like rain now, it was almost certain to rain later, and so it would be much safer just to sit in the garden with a book. Roger, in desperation, would place a large black paw on the gate, and then look at me, lifting one side of his upper lip, displaying his white teeth in a lopsided, ingratiating grin, his stump working itself into a blur of excitement. This was his trump card, for he knew I could never resist his ridiculous grin.

8 January

Today's dog is Kashtanka, the titular character of an 1887 short story by Russian writer Anton Chekhov. Kashtanka is a fox-like little mongrel who becomes lost after being separated from her owner. She finds herself taken in by a stranger and becomes part of his troupe of performing animals, which includes a cat, a pig and a goose called Ivan Ivanovich.

9 January

English poet William Robert Spencer was born on this day in 1769. Today's dog is Gelert, the tragic hero of Spencer's poem 'Beth Gelert, or the Grave of a Greyhound'. The poem describes how Gelert's master Llewellyn returns from a hunt to find his faithful hound with a blood-stained muzzle, and his young son apparently missing from his bloodied bed. Thinking Gelert has eaten his boy, Llewellyn stabs the dog – only to discover his son safely hidden, unharmed, and a dead wolf lying nearby. After realizing his terrible error, Llewellyn builds a magnificent grave for his loyal and brave dog.

> Ah! what was then Llewellyn's pain,
> For now the truth was clear:
> The gallant's hound the wolf had slain,
> To save Llewellyn's heir.

10 January

Samuel Dashiell Hammett, author of the 1934 detective novel *The Thin Man,* died on this day in 1961. Today's dog is Asta, the lively Schnauzer owned by the novel's protagonists, Nick and Nora Charles.

> Asta jumped up and punched me in the belly with her front feet. Nora, at the other end of the leash, said: 'She's had a swell afternoon – knocked over a table of toys at Lord & Taylor's, scared a fat woman silly by licking her leg in Saks's, and has been patted by three policemen.'

11 January

Thomas Hardy died on this day in 1928. Today's dog is his beloved fox terrier Wessex, named after the fictional area the author created to feature in his literary works. Wessex – rumoured to be fond of the radio and something of a nightmare at mealtimes – now lies under a headstone that reads: 'The famous dog Wessex: faithful, unflinching'.

12 January

American writer Jack London was born on this day in 1876. His 1903 novel *The Call of the Wild* tells the story of Buck, a dog who is stolen and sold to be a sled dog in Alaska. As Buck learns to navigate the harsh environment, he grows stronger and braver, and begins to feel more drawn to the wilderness. He becomes the companion of a kind man named John Thornton, who rescues Buck from a cruel prospector, but after Thornton's camp is attacked by Native Americans, Buck finds himself the only survivor, alone in the wild.

> Night came on, and a full moon rose high over the trees into the sky, lighting the land till it lay bathed in ghostly day. And with the coming of the night, brooding and mourning by the pool, Buck became alive to a stirring of the new life in the forest [...]. He stood up, listening and scenting. From far away drifted a faint, sharp yelp, followed by a chorus of similar sharp yelps. As the moments passed the yelps grew closer and closer. Again Buck knew them

as things heard in that other world which persisted in his memory. He walked to the centre of the open space and listened. It was the call, the many-noted call, sounding more luringly and compellingly than before. And as never before, he was ready to obey. John Thornton was dead. The last tie was broken. Man and the claims of man no longer bound him.

13 January

Irish writer James Joyce died on this day in 1941. Unfortunately, after being attacked by a dog as a small child, Joyce remained afraid of dogs all his life, and his dislike of canines can often be seen on the page. Today's dog – with apologies to Mr Joyce – is Garryowen of *Ulysses*, the rather vicious canine companion of the character known only as 'The Citizen'.

So we turns into Barney Kiernan's and there, sure enough, was the citizen up in the corner having a great confab with himself and that bloody mangy mongrel, Garryowen, and he waiting for what the sky would drop in the way of drink.

—There he is, says I, in his gloryhole, with his cruiskeen lawn and his load of papers, working for the cause.

The bloody mongrel let a grouse out of him would give you the creeps. Be a corporal work of mercy if someone would take the life of that bloody dog. I'm told for a fact he ate a good part of the breeches off a constabulary man in Santry that came round one time with a blue paper about a licence.

14 January

Greyfriars Bobby was a fiercely loyal terrier who died on this day in 1872, after spending 14 years at Greyfriars Kirkyard in Edinburgh, where he was said to be guarding the grave of his deceased master John Gray. He had become famous among local citizens for his faithfulness, and after his death he was buried in the same graveyard, close to his master. His story has been immortalized in several books, including *Greyfriars Bobby* by Eleanor Atkinson.

'A gude nicht to ye, Bobby.'

They could not see the little dog, but they knew he was there. They knew now that he would still be there when they could see him no more—his body a part of the soil, his memory a part of all that was held dear and imperishable in that old garden of souls. They could go up to the lodge and look at his famous collar, and they would have his image in bronze on the fountain. And sometime, when the mysterious door opened for them, they might see Bobby again, a sonsie doggie running on the green pastures and beside the still waters, at the heels of his shepherd master, for:

If there is not more love in this world than there is room for in God's heaven, Bobby would just have 'gaen awa' hame.'

15 January

From one faithful dog to another: today's canine is Argos, the four-legged friend of Odysseus in Homer's *Odyssey*. When Odysseus leaves to fight in the Trojan War, he leaves behind Argos, whom he had been training as a hunting dog. When his master fails to return, the poor dog is neglected. Still, he waits, growing old and emaciated – and when Odysseus finally returns twenty years on, in disguise as a beggar and unable to acknowledge the old hound for fear of revealing his true identity, Argos recognizes him at once.

> Abandoned there, and half destroyed with flies,
> old Argos lay.
> But when he knew he heard
> Odysseus' voice nearby, he did his best
> to wag his tail, nose down, with flattened ears,
> having no strength to move nearer his master.

Having at last laid eyes on his much-loved master, old Argos dies – but this tender moment between man and dog highlights the bittersweet nature of Odysseus's homecoming.

16 January

Today's dog is Enzo, the canine narrator of Garth Stein's *The Art of Racing in the Rain.* Enzo believes that if he prepares properly, he will be reincarnated as a human in his next life. Here, he muses on how having lived as a dog will make him a better human.

> Here's why I will be a good person. Because I listen. I cannot speak, so I listen very well. I never interrupt, I never deflect the course of the conversation with a comment of my own. People, if you pay attention to them, change the direction of one another's conversations constantly. It's like having a passenger in your car who suddenly grabs the steering wheel and turns you down a side street. [...] Learn to *listen*! I beg of you. Pretend you are a dog like me and listen to other people rather than steal their stories.

17 January

Anne Brontë was born on this day in 1820. Today's dog is her beloved spaniel, Flossy, who often accompanied her mistress on walks across the moors, and features in sketches and paintings made by Anne and her sisters.

18 January

Writer and poet Rudyard Kipling died on this day in 1936. In his honour, today's canine is Akela, 'the great grey Lone Wolf, who led all the pack by strength and cunning'. Akela appears in Kipling's famous 1894 novel *The Jungle Book*, and uses his influence as the head of the wolfpack to ensure the man-cub Mowgli is adopted by the wolves instead of being handed over to the tiger Shere Khan. Later in the novel, he and another wolf, Grey Brother, help Mowgli to defeat the tiger once and for all.

19 January

American writer Edgar Allan Poe was born on this day in 1809. Although he is best known for his spooky tales and Gothic poems, today's dog comes from his short story 'The Business Man', which tells the tale of Peter Proffit and the lengths he goes to in order to make money, including running a shoe-shining scam with the help of a dog named Pompey.

> My location, to be sure, was an excellent one, being central, and I had capital [shoe] blacking and brushes. My little dog, too, was quite fat and up to all varieties of snuff. He had been in the trade a long time and, I may say, understood it. Our general routine was this: Pompey, having rolled himself well in the mud, sat upon end at the shop door, until he observed a dandy approaching in bright boots. He then proceeded to meet him, and

gave the Wellingtons a rub or two with his wool. Then the dandy swore very much, and looked about for a boot-black. There I was, full in view, with blacking and brushes. It was only a minute's work, and then came a sixpence. This did moderately well for a time – in fact, I was not avaricious, but my dog was. I allowed him a third of the profit, but he was advised to insist upon half. This I couldn't stand – so we quarrelled and parted.

20 January

Dogs don't know what they look like. Dogs don't even know what size they are. No doubt it's our fault, for breeding them into such weird shapes and sizes. My brother's dachshund, standing tall at eight inches, would attack a Great Dane in the full conviction that she could tear it apart. When a little dog is assaulting its ankles the big dog often stands there looking confused – 'Should I eat it? Will it eat me? I *am* bigger than it, aren't I?' But then the Great Dane will come and try to sit in your lap and mash you flat, under the impression that it is a Peke-a-poo.

– Ursula K Le Guin, 'Dogs, Cats and Dancers – Thoughts about Beauty'

21 January

So I envy animals. Dogs especially, because nothing smells bad to them.

– Jonathan Franzen, *Purity*

22 January

Poet Lord Byron was born on this day in 1788. He is almost as renowned for his lively love life as he is for his striking Romantic poetry, but today we are paying tribute to one of his greatest loves: his dog, Boatswain. After the dog's death in 1808, Byron had him buried in a tomb on his estate at Newstead Abbey (incidentally, Boatswain's tomb is larger than the one Byron would eventually occupy himself), and wrote this epitaph, which is carved on the dog's monument:

When some proud Son of Man returns to Earth,
Unknown to Glory, but upheld by Birth,
The sculptor's art exhausts the pomp of woe,
And stories urns record who rests below.
When all is done, upon the Tomb is seen,
Not what he was, but what he should have been.
But the poor Dog, in life the firmest friend,
The first to welcome, foremost to defend,
Whose honest heart is still his Master's own,
Who labours, fights, lives, breathes for him alone,
Unhonour'd falls, unnotic'd all his worth,
Deny'd in heaven the Soul he held on earth:
While man, vain insect! hopes to be forgiven,
And claims himself a sole exclusive heaven.

Oh man! thou feeble tenant of an hour,
Debas'd by slavery, or corrupt by power.
Who knows thee well must quit thee with disgust,
Degraded mass of animated dust!
Thy love is lust, thy friendship all a cheat,

Thy smiles hypocrisy, thy words deceit!
By nature vile, ennoble but by name,
Each kindred brute might bid thee blush for shame.
Ye! who perchance behold this simple urn,
Pass on – it honours none you wish to mourn.
To mark a friend's remains these stones arise;
I never knew but one – and here he lies.

23 January

If you don't own a dog, at least one, there is not necessarily anything wrong with you, but there may be something wrong with your life.

– Roger A Caras, *A Celebration of Dogs*

24 January

American writer Edith Wharton was born on this day in 1862. She famously adored dogs, and kept many through her life, including Mimi, Jules, Toto and Miza, all of whom are buried at her former home The Mount in Massachusetts. In a letter to her friend Charles Eliot Norton, Wharton wrote:

> Staunch and faithful little lovers that they are, they give back a hundred fold every sign of love one ever gives them – & it mitigates the pang of losing them to know how very happy a little affection has made them.

25 January

Today is Burns Night, marking the birthday of Scottish poet Robert Burns, born on this day in 1759. To mark the occasion, please enjoy these lines from his poem 'The Twa Dogs', presented as a dialogue between a gentleman's dog, Caesar, and a ploughman's collie, Luath. After a long discussion about poverty, inequality and happiness, the two dogs part ways.

By this, the sun was out of sight,
An' darker gloaming brought the night;
The bum-clock humm'd wi' lazy drone;
The kye stood rowtin i' the loan;
When up they gat an' shook their lugs,
Rejoic'd they werena men but dogs;
An' each took aff his several way,
Resolv'd to meet some ither day.

26 January

Jasper [was] a might good dog too; he wa'n't no common dog, he wa'n't no mongrel; he was a composite. A composite dog is a dog that's made up of all the valuable qualities that's in the dog breed – kind of a syndicate; and a mongrel is made up of the riffraff that's left over. That Jasper was one of the most wonderful dogs you ever see.

– Mark Twain, *Autobiography of Mark Twain Vol 3*

27 January

He thinks people's dreams are made out of what they do all day. The same way a dog that runs after rabbits will dream of rabbits. It's what you do that makes your soul, not the other way around.

– Barbara Kingsolver, *Animal Dreams*

28 January

French writer Colette was born on this day in 1873. Although she is often thought of as a cat person (and it's true that felines frequently feature in her work), she had a much-adored French bulldog she named Toby-Chien (his name is sometimes written as Toby-Dog, but Toby-Chien is much more chic, and therefore much more Colette). She was photographed several times with her little muse, and he also played a starring role in her book *Barks and Purrs*, which imagined a series of conversations between him and a Maltese cat, Kiki-the-Demure.

KIKI-THE-DEMURE
I have a right to everything.

TOBY-DOG
To everything? And I?

KIKI-THE-DEMURE
I don't imagine you lack anything, do you?

TOBY-DOG
Ah, I don't know. Sometimes in my very happiest moments, I feel like crying. My eyes grow dim, my heart seems to choke me. I would like to be sure, in such times of anguish, that everybody loves me; that there is nowhere in the world a sad dog behind a closed door, that no evil will ever come …

29 January

Polish writer Olga Tokarczuk was born on this day in 1962. The following extract comes from her much celebrated novel *Drive Your Plow Over the Bones of the Dead,* which was shortlisted for the 2019 International Booker Prize. Dogs – and animals in general – feature prominently in the novel, a mystery that opens with an older woman, Janina, and her friend Oddball discovering that their neighbour, whom they call Big Foot, has died, leaving behind his dog and a series of unanswered questions.

> I said hello to Big Foot's Dog, who had been resident at Oddball's for the past few hours. She recognised me and was clearly pleased to see me. She wagged her tail – by now she'd probably forgotten about the time when she'd run away from me. Some Dogs can be silly, just like people, and this Dog was clearly one of them.

30 January

Today's dog is Bilbo, one of the two rescue dogs adopted by Eileen Battersby, whose stories she shared in the memoir *Ordinary Dogs: A Story of Two Lives.*

Bilbo tugged like a small husky. As for me, I was not a natural walker: I had always run, cycled or ridden horses, other people's until I had my own. Running with Bilbo was never going to work; a runner is a poor dog walker. We like to run onwards with no diversions. The dog has other ideas. [...] If I tried to jog along with him, he became excited, wheeling about and wrapping the leash around my legs. It was better to walk sedately; I could go running later, alone.

31 January

English novelist and playwright John Galsworthy died on this day in 1933. Today's dog is his beloved canine companion, Chris the spaniel.

Each August, till he was six, he was sent for health, and the assuagement of his hereditary instincts, up to a Scotch shooting, where he carried many birds in a very tender manner. Once he was compelled by Fate to remain there nearly a year; and we went up ourselves to fetch him home. Down the long avenue toward the keeper's cottage we walked: It was high autumn; there had been frost already, for the ground was fine with red and yellow leaves; and presently we saw himself coming; professionally questing among those leaves, and preceding his dear keeper with the businesslike self-containment of a sportsman; not too fat, glossy as a raven's wing, swinging his ears and sporran like a little Highlander. We approached him silently. Suddenly his nose went up from its imagined trail, and he came rushing at our legs. From him, as a garment drops from a man, dropped all his strange soberness; he became in a single instant one fluttering eagerness. He leaped from life to life in one bound, without hesitation, without regret. Not one sigh, not one look back, not the faintest token of gratitude or regret at leaving those good people who had tended him for a whole year, buttered oat-cake for him, allowed him to choose each night exactly where he would sleep. No, he just marched out beside us, as close as ever he could get, drawing us on in spirit, and not even attending to the scents, until the lodge gates were passed.

FEBRUARY

It might feel like it's been winter for approximately 4,000 years, but as February arrives, we will notice that the days are starting to get ever so slightly longer. It's still a cold and miserable month, though, so the dogs we'll be meeting will do their best to lift our spirits. We'll encounter no fewer than three of Dickens's dogs (7, 13 and 16 February), from the meanest to the sweetest. We'll also come across an Afghan hound (5 February), a standard poodle with a fondness for travelling (27 February) and more than a few Dalmatians (14 February).

Moveable feasts

CHINESE NEW YEAR: The first day of the Chinese New Year begins on the new moon between 21 January and 20 February. Each year is assigned an animal according to the Chinese zodiac, and these repeat in a 12-year cycle. You will be delighted to know that one of these animals is the dog, which is associated with loyalty, honesty and faithfulness.

The next Year of the Dog will start in February 2030.

1 February

Novelist Muriel Spark (author of *The Prime of Miss Jean Brodie*, among many others) was born on this day in 1918. As well as longer works, she was a talented writer of short stories, and today's dogs come from her short story 'Alice Long's Dachshunds', which was published in the *New Yorker* in 1967. It depicts a young girl, Mamie, walking the dogs owned by her father's former employer: five 'little paddling, waddling' Dachshunds named Mitzi, Fritzi, Blitzi, Ritzi and Kitzy.

> The dogs go about together and sometimes all answer at once when Alice Long calls one of their names. Mamie does not know them apart. They vary slightly in size, fatness, and in the black scars on their brown coats.

A word of warning: dog-lovers may not like the story's ending …

2 February

Today's dog is Carlo, companion and muse to poet Emily Dickinson. He is thought to have been a brown Newfoundland, and may have been named in honour of the pointer owned by St John Rivers in *Jane Eyre*. In February 1863, Dickinson wrote to her friend T W Higgison describing Carlo as 'my shaggy ally'.

3 February

American writer Gertrude Stein was born on this day in 1874. She shared several dogs with her partner Alice B Toklas – including more than one white poodle named Basket. In 1935, she wrote to her friend about the first Basket, describing him with great love and affection.

> [H]e is a darling and I do hope someday you and he will meet, he is perhaps too friendly he errs on that side, and even when another dog bites him, he is convinced that it was an accident, he cannot accept it as intentional [...] He is a happy fool, and a great comfort.

4 February

Today's dog is Zero, canine companion of Jack Bagthorpe, the only 'ordinary' member of the super-talented Bagthorpe family, whose antics fill Helen Cresswell's YA novel series *The Bagthorpe Saga.*

> It was Mr Bagthorpe who had given him his name. 'If there was anything less than Zero, that hound would be it,' he had said. It was not a good name to have to go through life with, and Jack sometimes wondered if it affected Zero, and gave him an inferiority complex. He spent a lot of time trying to build Zero's confidence, because he could tell by the way his ears drooped when he was getting sad and undermined.

5 February

Comedy writer and all-round entertainer Frank Muir was born on this day in 1920. Today's dog is his creation What-a-Mess, star of a series of children's books (and later an animated series). What-a-Mess, whose real name is Prince Amir of Kinjan, is a scruffy Afghan hound with a tendency to get into messy scrapes.

6 February

Children's writer Joyce Lankester Brisley was born on this day in 1896. Today's dog is Toby, a sweet little black-and-white terrier who features in Lankester Brisley's beloved *Milly-Molly-Mandy* series.

> When she came to the gate Toby the dog capered up, looking very excited at the thought of a walk. But Milly-Molly-Mandy eyes him solemnly and said: 'Trowel for Farver, eggs for Muvver, string for Grandpa, red wool for Grandma, chicken-feed for Uncle, needles for Aunty. No, Toby, you mustn't come now, I've too much to think about. But I promise to take you for a walk when I come back!'

7 February

Charles Dickens was born on this day in 1812. In his honour, today's dog is Jip from his 1850 novel *David Copperfield.* Jip is the beloved companion of young David's love interest, Dora Spenlow, and she has a habit of involving the pooch in every conversation.

> '[Miss Murdstone] is a tiresome creature,' said Dora pouting. 'I can't think what Papa can have been about, when he chose such a vexatious thing to be my companion. Who wants a protector! I am sure *I* don't want a protector. Jip can protect me a great deal better than Miss Murdstone – can't you, Jip dear?'
>
> He only winked lazily, when she kissed his ball of a head.
>
> 'Papa calls her my confidential friend, but I am sure she is no such thing – is she, Jip? We are not going to confide in any such cross people, Jip and I. We mean to bestow our confidence where we like, and to find our own friends, instead of having them found out for us – don't we, Jip?'
>
> Jip made a comfortable noise in answer, a little like a tea-kettle when it sings.

We will be meeting more Dickens-related dogs on 13 and 16 February.

8 February

Novelist Iris Murdoch died on this day in 1999. In her honour, today's dog is Zed, who appears in her 1983 novel *The Philosopher's Pupil.*

> [Zed] was a *papillon*, one of the smallest of all dogs, a little dainty long-haired black and white thing with floppy plumy ears and a jaunty plumy tail, and the very darkest of blue-brown shining amused clever eyes. Adam had named him. Asked why, he had replied, 'Because we are Alpha and Omega.'

9 February

American activist and novelist Alice Walker was born on this day in 1944. Today's dog is her beloved black Labrador retriever Marley, named after Bob Marley. In her essay 'Crimes Against Dog', Walker describes choosing Marley as a puppy and later bringing her home. On the drive, the puppy climbed out of her basket and into Walker's lap.

> From my lap she began journeying up my stomach to my chest. By the time we approached the bridge she'd discovered my dreadlocks and began climbing them. As we rolled into the city she had climbed all the way to the back of my neck and settled herself there between my neck and the headrest. Once there, she snoozed.

10 February

American writer Laura Ingalls Wilder died on this day in 1957. To mark the date, our dog today is Jack, the 'brindle bulldog' who appears in her *Little House on the Prairie* books. While crossing a creek on their travels, the family are separated from their loyal Jack, and young Laura is distraught. As they make camp that night, they hear wolves howling in the distance.

> When wolves howled in the Big Woods, Laura had always known that Jack would not let them hurt her. A lump swelled hard in her throat and her nose smarted. She winked fast and did not cry.
>
> [...] Deep in the dark beyond the firelight, two green lights were shining near the ground. They were eyes.
>
> Cold ran up Laura's backbone, her scalp crinkled, her hair stood up. The green lights moved; one winked out, then the other winked out, then both shone steadily, coming nearer.
>
> 'Look, Pa, look!' Laura said. 'A wolf!'
>
> [...] Pa slowly walked toward those eyes. And slowly along the ground the eyes crawled toward him. Laura could see the animal in the edge of the dark. It was a tawny animal and brindled. Then Pa shouted and Laura screamed.
>
> The next thing she knew she was trying to hug a jumping, panting, wriggling Jack, who lapped her face and hands with his warm wet tongue. She couldn't hold him. He leaped and wriggled from her to Pa and Ma and back again.

11 February

Today marks the International Day of Women and Girls in Science. To mark the occasion, our dog is Six-Thirty: admittedly not a woman or a girl, and really only science adjacent, but still the most loyal and loved companion of scientist-turned-cooking-show-host Elizabeth Zott in Bonnie Garmus's bestselling novel *Lessons in Chemistry*. Six-Thirty – named after the time he followed his new owner home after she walked past the alley where he was lurking – is a gentle, highly intelligent dog with a remarkable ability to understand language.

> Many people go to breeders to find a dog, and others to the pound, but sometimes, especially when it's really meant to be, the right dog finds you.

12 February

American author Judy Blume was born on this day in 1938. Among her many beloved books is *Tales of a Fourth Grade Nothing*, part of her 'Fudge' series, which follows the lives of nine-year-old Peter and his infuriating little brother Farley, known as Fudge. When Fudge swallows his beloved pet turtle Dribble, Peter is understandably distraught. His parents try to soothe his loss by buying him a puppy, whom Peter – appropriately enough – names Turtle.

13 February

Today's dog is Poodles – who, despite his name, is not a poodle, but a friendly mongrel who appears in Charles Dickens's essay collection *The Uncommercial Traveller*. Dickens describes how Poodles has become a sort of unofficial therapy dog at the children's hospital, keeping the patients company and lightening the atmosphere with his friendly antics.

> And trotting about among the beds, on familiar terms with all the patients, was a comical mongrel dog called Poodles. This comical dog (quite a tonic in himself) was found characteristically starving at the door of the institution, and was taken in and fed, and has lived here ever since. An admirer of his mental endowments has presented him with a collar bearing the legend, 'Judge not Poodles by external appearances'. He was merrily wagging his tail on a boy's pillow when he made this modest appeal to me.

14 February

Today is Valentine's Day, and to mark the occasion we celebrate the love of two Dalmatians – not Pongo and Missis, but another spotted couple who also appear in Dodie Smith's *The Hundred and One Dalmatians*: Perdita and Prince.

> [Perdita's] way to the village lay across the common, where she saw a large, handsome car which had been driven on to the grass. A group of people were having

> a picnic – and with them was a superb liver-spotted Dalmatian. [...] He wore a magnificent collar and was being offered a piece of chicken by a richly dressed lady. At that moment, he saw Perdita.
>
> It was love at first sight. Without even bothering to eat the chicken, he came bounding to her, and they were away into a wood together before anybody could stop them. Here they made swift arrangements for their marriage, promising to love each other always.

The new lovers are sadly separated soon after, but ultimately reunited – becoming part of the 101-strong pack.

15 February

> Dogs are wise. They crawl away into a quiet corner and lick their wounds and do not rejoin the world until they are whole once more.
>
> – Agatha Christie, *The Moving Finger*

16 February

Like many of his works, Charles Dickens's *Oliver Twist* was first published in serial format – and the first part of the serial was published in February 1837. With this in mind, today's dog is Bull's-eye, the terrier owned by the villainous Bill Sikes. Dickens describes the hound as 'having faults of temper in common with his owner'.

In the obscure parlour of a low public-house, in the filthiest part of Little Saffron Hill; a dark and gloomy den, where a flaring gas-light burnt all day in the winter-time; and where no ray of sun ever shone in the summer: there sat, brooding over a little pewter measure and a small glass, strongly impregnated with the smell of liquor, a man in a velveteen coat, drab shorts, half-boots and stockings, whom even by that dim light no experienced agent of the police would have hesitated to recognise as Mr William Sikes. At his feet sat a white-coated, red-eyed dog; who occupied himself, alternately, in winking at his master with both eyes at the same time; and in licking a large, fresh cut on one side of his mouth, which appeared to be the result of some recent conflict.

17 February

In this diary entry from 1989, Australian writer Helen Garner describes her grief following the death of her family's pet dog.

The unusual colour of her fur – a silvery grey that almost shone in the dark. I got out my photo albums and looked for her. Not many where she was the star, but often a corner of her was visible in a picture of something else: a nose, a paw, a length of silvery back. Cried for her terrible faithfulness, her loneliness and confusion when our household broke up, how she would escape and trot the five kms to F's, missing death on the roads. And the way she used to flick up her hind legs in a gay little gambol when she set out with us on a walk.

18 February

Pilot was a small puppy, but even then he had the most enormous paws: they knew the breed could get very large, but nothing had prepared them for the extraordinary size to which Pilot eventually grew. Every time they thought he couldn't get any bigger, he did: sometimes it was almost funny to see how disproportionately small he made everything around him look, their house and their car and even one another.

'I'm unusually tall,' he said, 'and sometimes you get sick of being taller than everyone else. But when I stood next to Pilot, I felt normal.'

– Rachel Cusk, *Kudos*

19 February

American writer Amy Tan, author of the 1989 bestseller *The Joy Luck Club*, was born on this day in 1952. She is known for her love of Yorkshire terriers, and has enjoyed the faithful companionship of several during her lifetime, including Bubba Zo, Lilli, Bobo and Frankie.

20 February

Irish writer Sally Rooney was born on this day in 1991. Today's dog is the charming Alexei from her bestselling 2024 novel *Intermezzo*, which explores the relationship between two very different brothers following their father's death. The book is profound, moving and at times steeped in sorrow – so sweet little Alexei provides some welcome light.

> Ivan notices people looking at Alexei, children for example, pointing at the dog and smiling. Alexei, relishing the attention, lifts his paws elegantly, cock of the walk, even holding his head at a jaunty angle while they make their way down the street. [...] Only now, attempting for the first time in nearly a year to walk his dog through a busy urban environment, does Ivan remember what an embarrassing little showboat Alexei can be in front of people.

21 February

American novelist Jonathan Safran Foer was born on this day in 1977. In his honour, today's dog is Sammy Davis, Junior, Junior from his 2002 book *Everything is Illuminated.* Sammy Davis, Junior, Junior is a guide dog – or, as the book's characters rather unceremoniously refer to her, a 'seeing-eye bitch'.

> And I still haven't mentioned that Grandfather demanded to bring Sammy Davis, Junior, Junior along. That was another thing. [...] Finally my father yielded, although it was agreed that Sammy Davis, Junior, Junior must don a special shirt that Father would have fabricated, which would say: OFFICIOUS SEEING-EYE BITCH OF HERITAGE TOURING. This was so she would appear professional.

22 February

To focus, I think of how dogs are witnesses. How they are present for our most private moments, how they are there when we think of ourselves as alone. They witness our quarrels, our tears, our struggles, our fears, and all of our secret behaviours that we have to hide from our fellow humans. They witness without judgement.

– Steven Rowley, *Lily and the Octopus*

23 February

Today's dog is Petitcreiu, the beloved companion of the legendary Isolde. While most dogs in myth and legend tend to be powerful hunting beasts or brave fighters, Petitcreiu is a lapdog – but he is a very special one. He wears a bell whose chime causes whoever hears it to instantly forget their sorrow. Tristan gifts Petitcreiu to his beloved Isolde to try and ease her pain at their parting, but she decides to remove the bell – she would rather feel her pain than forget her love for Tristan. Even without the magic bell, Petitcreiu brings his mistress great comfort – as all dogs do.

24 February

Today's dog is Lydia, the drooling Great Dane who brings comfort to the heartbroken narrator of Monica Heisey's 2023 hit novel *Really Good, Actually*.

Lydia was a well-behaved dope with no idea how huge she was, deferring instantly to the much smaller, more confident dogs that strolled right up to get in her face or sniff her butthole.

25 February

In his strikingly original novel *City*, American sci-fi writer Clifford D Simak imagines an exceedingly introspective, futuristic world where humans abandon the cities and gradually fade out, while a dog civilization takes over the urban spaces. The novel is made up of a series of legends passed down by the dogs from generation to generation.

> These are the stories that the Dogs tell when fires burn high and the wind is from the north. Then each family circle gathers at the hearthstone and the pups sit silently and listen and when the story's done they ask many questions:
>
> 'What is Man?' they'll ask.
>
> Or perhaps: 'What is a city?'
>
> Or: 'What is a war?'
>
> There is no positive answer to any of these questions.

26 February

While musing on the nature of the soul in her journal in February 1926, Virginia Woolf made reference to her dog, Grizzle.

> And the truth is, one can't write directly about the soul. Looked at, it vanishes; but look at the ceiling, at Grizzle,

at the cheaper beasts in the Zoo which are exposed to walkers in Regent's Park, and the soul slips in.

27 February

American writer John Steinbeck was born on this day in 1902. Today's dog is Charley, the standard poodle who accompanied Steinbeck on a 1960 road trip that he then recounted in his travelogue *Travels with Charley.*

> For when Charley is groomed and clipped and washed he is as pleased with himself as is any man with a good tailor, or a woman newly patinaed by a beauty parlour; all of whom can believe they are like that clear through. Charley's combed columns of legs were noble things, his cap of silver blue fur was rakish, and he carried the pompom of his tail like the baton of a bandmaster. A wealth of combed and clipped moustache gave him the appearance and attitude of a French rake of the nineteenth century, and incidentally concealed his crooked front teeth. [...] If manners maketh man, then manner and grooming maketh poodle.

28 February

We will be meeting more of Jane Austen's literary pooches later on (18 July and 16 December), but today's dogs come to us from her 1817 novel *Northanger Abbey.* These hunting dogs are probably the only bearable thing about the self-absorbed John Thorpe.

[T]he rest of his conversation, or rather talk, began and ended with himself and his own concerns. He told her of horses which he had bought for a trifle and sold for incredible sums; or racing matches, in which his judgement had infallibly foretold the winner; of shooting parties, in which he had killed more birds (though without having one good shot) than all his companions together; and described to her some famous day's sport, with the fox-hounds, in which his foresight and skill in directing the dogs had repaired the mistakes of the most experiences huntsman, and in which the boldness of his riding, though it had never endangered his own life, had been constantly leading others into difficulties which he calmly concluded had broken the necks of many.

Little as Catherine was in the habit of judging for herself, and unfixed as were her general notions of what men ought to be, she could not entirely repress a doubt, while she bore with the effusions of his endless conceit, of his being altogether completely agreeable.

29 February

Harriet was opening her mouth to say No, when she looked at Mr Pomfret, and her heart softened. He had the appeal of a very young dog of a very large breed – a kind of amiable absurdity.

– Dorothy L Sayers, *Gaudy Night*

MARCH

Spring is here at last: the air is warmer, the days are longer and gardens are starting to fill with flowers (although not if 28 March's pooch has anything to do with it). As the world wakes from its wintry slumber, it's an excellent time to lace up your walking shoes and take your four-legged friend out for a good long stomp.

This month's canines include foxes, from the courageous (1 March) to the crafty (29 March), and wolves, both orchestral (5 March) and wild (23 March). There are some moments that will tug at the heartstrings (18, 20 and 31 March in particular), but the delightful Bibbles, whom we meet on 30 March, will soothe any troubled soul.

Moveable feasts

WORLD BOOK DAY: World Book Day takes place on the first Thursday in March, and is a great opportunity to get out the fancy-dress box and put together a costume based on one of your favourite fictional characters. If you're lucky enough to have a canine companion, why not dress up together as one of the iconic literary duos in this book: Dorothy and Toto, Tintin and Snowy, Odysseus and Argos … the list goes one.

MOTHER'S DAY: In the UK, Mother's Day is celebrated on the fourth Sunday of Lent, meaning it usually falls in March or April (in the US, however, it is marked on the second Sunday in May). One of the best-known bookish dog mothers is Missis from Dodie Smith's *The Hundred and One Dalmatians* (also 14 February and 3 May), who with her husband Pongo has a beautiful litter of puppies – and then goes to desperate lengths to rescue them from the evil clutches of Cruella de Vil.

1 March

The start of a month is all about new beginnings, so in that spirit, today's canine is Fox, one of the beloved heroes of Colin Dann's children's book *The Animals of Farthing Wood,* which sees a group of animals band together in search of a new home when their habitat is destroyed. In the extract below, the dashing, brave and clever Fox is chosen by Badger to lead the animals on their journey.

> 'We've decided Toad is to be our guide. Kestrel and Owl will go ahead as scouts. But we need a leader; someone who is courageous and able to make quick decisions. I can't think of anyone better than you, Fox.'
>
> Fox showed his appreciation by wagging his tail.

2 March

Writer and illustrator of children's books Dr Seuss was born on this day in 1904. To continue with yesterday's foxy theme, today's dog is his 1965 creation *Fox in Socks*. In the book, we meet the characters Fox and Knox, and follow them on a tongue-twister-heavy series of encounters with socks, a box, blocks ...

You get the idea.

3 March

Today is International Writers' Day, and to mark the occasion today's dog is the diminutive pooch owned by writing teacher Ursula (aka Fosco) in Mona Awad's *Bunny*. The darkly comic novel follows aspiring writer Samantha as she studies for an MFA in Creative Writing and tries to avoid her classmates, the twee yet sinister young women Samanta calls the Bunnies.

> Meanwhile, Fosco's sweatered terrier yips at her heels or else runs idiotic circles around us. She brought it to every class last semester. The Bunnies would coo at the creature for a good fifteen minutes at the start of class while I sat there, pretending to read whatever random, formally experimental text Fosco had assigned that week.

4 March

Today's dog is Kep, the wise collie who appears in Beatrix Potter's *The Tale of Jemima Puddle-Duck*. When Jemima is tricked by a wily fox into laying her eggs in his shed, not realizing he intends to eat her and her ducklings, Kep figures out what is happening and hurries to the rescue. Such a good boy.

5 March

Russian composer Sergei Prokofiev died on this day in 1953. He composed *Peter and the Wolf*, a tale for children based on a Russian story, with each character brought to life by a different section of the orchestra as the tale is narrated. The titular wolf is represented by French horns.

6 March

English poet Elizabeth Barrett Browning was born on this day in 1806. She adored her dog Flush, who often featured in her letters, and even inspired Virginia Woolf to write a novel – *Flush: A Biography*. Although it is, on the surface, about the precious pet and his mistress, Woolf also used the work as an opportunity to pass social commentary on a number of issues, including feminism and class. The extract below describes the first meeting between poet and pooch:

> 'Oh, Flush!' said Miss Barrett. For the first time she looked him in the face. For the first time Flush looked at the lady lying on the sofa.
>
> Each was surprised. Heavy curls hung down on either side of Miss Barrett's face; large bright eyes shone out; a large mouth smiled. Heavy ears hung down on either side of Flush's face; his eyes, too, were large and bright: his mouth was wide. There was a likeness between them. As they gazed at each other each felt: Here I am – and then each felt: But how different! Hers was the pale

worn face of an invalid, cut off from air, light, freedom. His was the warm ruddy face of a young animal; instinct with health and energy. Broken asunder, yet made in the same mould, could it be that each completed what was dormant in the other? She might have been – all that; and he – But no. Between them lay the widest gulf that can separate one being from another. She spoke. He was dumb. She was woman; he was dog. Thus closely united, thus immensely divided, they gazed at each other. Then with one bound Flush sprang on to the sofa and laid himself where he was to lie forever – on the rug at Miss Barrett's feet.

7 March

Today's dog is Red, the beautiful Irish setter featured in Jim Kjelgaard's 1945 novel *Big Red.*

A shiny, silky red from nose to tail, the dog was trotting up the path Danny was walking down. His eyes were fixed on Danny, and his tail wagged gently a couple of times. Ten feet away he stood still, his finely chiselled head erect and his body rigid. Spellbound, Danny returned the dog's gaze. He knew dogs, having owned and hunted with hounds since he was old enough to do anything. The red dog was not a hound – Danny knew vaguely that it was called an Irish setter – but never before had he seen any dog that revealed at first glance all the qualities a dog should have.

8 March

If the story of Greyfriars Bobby (14 January) had you reaching for the tissues, you may need a fresh pack. Today's dog is Hachikō, an Akita dog who lived in Tokyo, Japan. His beloved owner was a professor at the university, and at the end of every day, Hachikō used to go to their local train station to greet his master after his commute. His owner died in May 1925 – but Hachikō continued to go to the station every day, patiently waiting for his master's train to arrive. He did this every day until his own death, on this day in 1935. The gentle pooch's unwavering loyalty made him a cultural icon, and he has been memorialized in statues, films and books, including *Hachikō Waits* by Lesléa Newman, illustrated by Machiyo Kodaira.

9 March

English writer Vita Sackville-West was born on this day in 1892. In her book *Faces: Profiles of Dogs,* she meditates on the different breeds and considers their attributes. While the book contains possibly the most accurate description of an Afghan hound ever written ('like somebody's elderly spinster aunt [...] Aunt Lavinia, who nourishes a secret passion for the Vicar'), today we focus on her wise words on mongrels.

> Alas, we can honour him with no history, no pedigree. He must speak for himself, with those great wistful eyes, as appealing as a lost child. Fortunately for him he

is well able to do so. I have owned, or been owned by, several mongrels in my time, and never have I known dogs more capable of falling on their feet.

10 March

Russian writer Mikhail Bulgakov died on this day in 1940. Although his famous work *The Master and Margarita* is better known for its feline contingent (and the chess-playing cat Behemoth does occupy a fair amount of chapter space), the novel's pages do also feature a dog or two. Today's dog is the Ace of Diamonds, a police dog whose reputation precedes him.

> And after a short time a group of investigating officials appeared at the theatre, accompanied by a sharp-eared, muscular dog the colour of cigarette ashes, with extremely intelligent eyes. An excited whisper ran throughout the building, spreading the information that the dog was none other than the famous Ace of Diamonds.

11 March

English writer Douglas Adams, best known for his *Hitchhiker's Guide to the Galaxy* books, was born on this day in 1952. Today's dog is Know-Nothing-Bozo, a slightly dense pooch who first appears in Adams's 1984 novel *So Long, and Thanks for All the Fish.* (Those wondering if Adams had access to a time machine should note that Know-Nothing-Bozo was meant to resemble Ronald Reagan, not, erm, someone else.)

> A small black wire-haired terrier ran out from behind a low wall and then, catching sight of Arthur, began to snarl.
>
> Now Arthur knew this dog, and he knew it well. It belonged to an advertising friend of his, and was called Know-Nothing-Bozo because the way its hair stood up on its head reminded people of the President of the United States of America [...] It was a stupid dog, could not even read an autocue, which was why some people had protested about its name, but it should at least have been able to recognise Arthur instead of standing there, hackles raised, as if Arthur was the most fearful apparition ever to intrude upon its feeble-witted life.

12 March

Jack Kerouac was born on this day in 1922. Today's dog, then, is Potchky, a cocker spaniel owned by his friend Lucien Carr. Kerouac famously wrote the manuscript for his seminal novel

On the Road in a three-week long burst of feverish activity in April 1951, typing the whole thing on one continuous scroll. And Potchky almost as famously took a liking to said scroll and ate the last part of it, devouring the final part of the Mexico trip and the epilogue. The original scroll bears a handwritten note by Kerouac in pencil near the eaten end: '-- DOG ATE (Potchky-a dog)'.

13 March

Today's dog is Copper, the canine protagonist of Daniel P Mannix's 1967 novel *The Fox and the Hound* (fans of the 1981 Disney adaptation should proceed with caution – the events of the novel are substantially different and a lot less cute). Copper is a talented hunting and tracking dog, a bloodhound with a powerful nose and total devotion to his master.

> Copper drank in the breeze in eager gulps. He had almost forgotten there was air like this, for the world came alive when the wind blew. It was a perfect scenting day, moist but not wet, with a light breeze. The ground felt warm under Copper's pads, but the air in his nostrils was deliciously cool. Joyfully he plunged into the white mist that rolled toward them as they entered the hollows, zigzagging to pick up the grand odours that told of rabbit,

pheasant, mouse and woodchuck. He was no longer old and tired and unneeded. Copper was young again, going hunting with the Master, and all he needed was the trace of a fox to make him completely happy.

14 March

David Wroblewski's 2008 novel *The Story of Edgar Sawtelle* is a retelling of Shakespeare's *Hamlet*, set on a dog-breeding farm in Wisconsin. Almondine, our dog of the day, is the loyal and intelligent companion of young Edgar, who is born mute. Almondine learns to understand sign language and sense Edgar's moods and needs, and becomes his voice. Below is their first meeting, when she realizes what her new role will be.

That was what the concern had been about, she realised.

The baby had no voice. It couldn't make a sound.

Almondine began to pant. She shifted her weight from one hip to the other, and as she looked on – and saw his mother continue to sleep – she finally understood: the thing that was going to happen was that her time for training was over, and now, at last, she had a job to do.

15 March

Dogs have important jobs, like barking when the doorbell rings, but cats have no function in a house whatsoever.

– W Bruce Cameron, *A Dog's Purpose*

16 March

Today's dog is Daisy, the beloved pet of the Pullman family in R J Palacio's 2012 children's novel *Wonder*. The book tells the story of ten-year-old August 'Auggie' Pullman, who was born with facial differences, and his older sister Olivia.

> August is the Sun. Me and Mom and Dad are planets orbiting the Sun. The rest of our family and friends are asteroids and comets floating around the planets orbiting the Sun. The only celestial body that doesn't orbit August the Sun is Daisy the dog, and that's only because to her little doggy eyes, August's face doesn't look very different from any other human's face. To Daisy, all our faces look alike, as flat and pale as the moon.

17 March

In honour of St Patrick's Day, today's dogs are Bran and Sceólang, the hounds of Irish folk hero Fionn mac Cumhaill. Loyal, brave and highly intelligent, they appear in numerous myths, and are said to be huge white beasts with crimson tails, purple haunches and blue feet. Legend has it that they were actually Fionn's cousins, as his aunt Uirne gave birth to them after she'd been transformed into a hound while pregnant.

18 March

American writer John Updike was born on this day in 1932. His poem 'Another Dog's Death' describes him sadly digging a grave for his ailing pet, and the way she gently keeps him company as he does so.

> The sun warmed her fur as she dozed and I dug;
> carved her a safe place while she protected me.

19 March

> 'The dog is a gentleman – I hope to go to his heaven, not man's.'
>
> – Mark Twain

20 March

Today's dog is the marvellously named Sir Hector Pinpin, a black Pomeranian owned by French novelist Émile Zola. Tragically, Sir Hector is said to have died of grief after his master was forced to flee to England in 1898 after being prosecuted for libel.

21 March

Today is World Poetry Day – and also marks the birthday of poet and satirist Alexander Pope, who was born on this day in 1688. To mark the occasion, today's dog is Shock, from Pope's narrative poem *The Rape of the Lock* (the title refers to a would-be suitor's theft of a lock of hair from the head of Belinda, Shock's mistress).

> When Shock, who thought she slept too long,
> Leapt up, and wak'd his mistress with his Tongue.

22 March

Japanese writer Haruki Murakami is well-known for his love of cats, but his novel *Sputnik Sweetheart* takes its name from the story of Laika, the dog who was sent into space aboard *Sputnik II* in 1957 by the Soviet Union. She became the first living being to leave the Earth's atmosphere, but there was no return journey.

> It made her think of Laika the dog. The man-made satellite streaking soundlessly across the blackness of outer space. The dark, lustrous eyes of the dog gazing out the tiny window. In the infinite loneliness of space, what could the dog possibly be looking at?

23 March

Sarah Hall's powerful 2015 novel *The Wolf Border* tells the story of Rachel, a wolf expert hired to help with a project involving the reintroduction of wild wolves to the Lake District.

> It comes between the bushes, as if bidden. It comes forward, mercilessly, towards her, paws lifting, fast, but not running. A word she will soon learn: *lope.* It is perfectly made: long legs, sheet chest, dressed for coldness in wraps of grey fur. [...] Long nose, the black tip twitching, short mane. A dog before dogs were invented. The god of all dogs. It is a creature so fine, she can hardly comprehend it.

24 March

French writer Jules Verne died on this day in 1905. Although best known for his adventure books *Around the World in Eighty Days, Journey to the Centre of the Earth* and *Twenty Thousand Leagues Under the Sea,* today's dog comes from one of his less-famous works, *Dick Sand, A Captain at Fifteen.* Dingo is 'a magnificent and robust beast, larger than the dogs of the Pyrenees', who is rescued from a shipwreck by another boat. He wears a collar engraved with the letters 'SV' – and, it appears, he knows how to read. A literary dog in every sense of the word.

[The letter cubes] were arranged on the deck, and little Jack was taking sometimes one, sometimes another, to make a word – a truly great labour.

Now, for some moments, Dingo was moving round the young child, when suddenly it stopped. Its eyes became fixed, its right paw was raised, its tail wagged convulsively. Then, suddenly throwing itself on one of the cubes, it seized it in its mouth and laid it on the deck a few steps from Jack.

This cube bore a large letter – the letter S.

'Dingo, well Dingo!' cried the little boy, who at first was afraid that his S was swallowed by the dog.

But Dingo returned, and, beginning the same performance again, it seized another cube, and went to lay it near the first.

This second cube was a V.

This time Jack gave a cry.

[...] Dingo knew its letters; Dingo knew how to read! That was very certain, that! Jack had seen it!

25 March

Arthur Conan Doyle's *The Hound of the Baskervilles* was published on this day in 1902, and depicts his legendary detective Sherlock Holmes investigating the legend of a fearsome demonic hound said to roam the wilds of Dartmoor. The creature is thought to be responsible for the deaths of many members of the local Baskerville family.

'I say, Watson,' said the baronet, 'what would Holmes say to this? How about that hour of darkness in which the power of evil is exalted?'

As if in answer to his words there rose suddenly out of the vast gloom of the moor that strange cry which I had already heard upon the borders of the great Grimpen Mire. It came with the wind through the silence of the night, a long, deep mutter, then a rising howl, and then the sad moan in which it died away. Again and again it sounded, the whole air throbbing with it, strident, wild, and menacing. The baronet caught my sleeve, and his face glimmered white through the darkness.

'Good heavens, what's that, Watson?'

'I don't know. It's a sound they have on the moor. I heard it once before.'

It died away, and an absolute silence closed in upon us. We stood straining our ears, but nothing came.

'Watson' said the baronet, 'it was the cry of a hound.'

26 March

British writer Diana Wynne Jones died on this day in 2011. In her honour, today's dog is Sirius, protagonist of her 1977 novel *Dogsbody*. Sirius is a star condemned to live on Earth as a dog after being accused of murder. Sirius has an important mission to carry out in order to regain his status as a celestial body – but being a dog turns out to be pretty distracting.

> His dog nature needed a free rein first. It cried out to examine every whiff and stink he passed, to raise its leg at every lamppost and corner, and to run up the pavement as it had seldom run before. When the joy of that subsided a little, Sirius remembered he had an errand. He turned and crossed the road.

27 March

Today marks World Theatre Day. To celebrate, enjoy this famous extract from Shakespeare's 1599 tragedy *Julius Caesar*, part of a soliloquy delivered by Mark Antony as he stands over Caesar's body following his assassination.

> And Caesar's spirit, ranging for revenge,
> With Ate by his side comes hot from hell,
> Shall in these confines with a monarch's voice
> Cry 'Havoc!' and let loose the dogs of war,
> That this foul deed shall smell above the earth
> With carrion men, groaning for burial.

28 March

Today's dog is Bendicò, a faithful Great Dane owned by the Prince of Salina in Giuseppe Tomasi di Lampedusa's 1958 classic *The Leopard.* Although Bendicò ultimately ends up in rug form, let's enjoy one of his livelier moments as he snuffles around the garden.

> He was sitting on a bench, inertly watching the devastation wrought by Bendicò in the flower beds; every now and again the dog would turn innocent eyes toward him as if asking for praise at labour done: fourteen carnations broken half off, half a hedge torn apart, an irrigation canal blocked. How human! 'Good! Bendicò, come here.' And the animal hurried up and put its earthy nostrils into his hand, anxious to show that it had forgiven this silly interruption of a fine job of work.

29 March

Our canines today are Isengrim the wolf and Reynard the fox, who appear in the *Ysengrimus*, a mock epic written by the poet Nivardus in around 1148 or 1149. Despite Isengrim's best efforts, he is frequently tricked and mocked by the wily Reynard. Both creatures appear in numerous fables and tales from the Middle Ages – and Reynard usually comes out on top.

30 March

Today's dog is Bibbles, star of D H Lawrence's poem of the same name, a 'little black dog' with a 'shoved-out jaw'. The tone of the poem is simultaneously delighted and reproachful as Lawrence describes the feeling known all too well by dog-owners everywhere: that the dog actually owns the human ('And even now, Bibbles, little Ma'am, it's you who appropriated me, not I you'). As the poem progresses, he describes with some jealousy how indiscriminately Bibbles bestows her love on others:

> You love to lap up affection, to wallow in it,
> And then turn tail to the next comer, for a new dollop.

Bibbles also makes an appearance in another of Lawrence's poems, 'The Blue Jay'.

31 March

> To old dogs the hour comes when, whistled by their master setting forth with his stick at dawn, they cannot spring after him. Then they stay in their kennel, or in their basket, though they are not chained, and listen to the steps dying away.
>
> – Samuel Beckett, *Malone Dies*

APRIL

We are now officially in springtime, with warmer weather, budding leaves and probably a few more April showers than we might strictly like. This month we'll be meeting the canine companions of some famous writers (12, 15 and 18 April), and encountering some truly terrifying mythological hounds (11 and 20 April). We'll also spend some time with a cartoon police dog (5 April), a wise fox (4 April) and a bulldog who likes hogging the duvet (29 April).

Moveable feasts

EASTER: The Christian festival of Easter typically falls between 22 March and 25 April, falling on the first Sunday after the full moon that occurs on or after the spring equinox. As a festival, it has more to do with rabbits and chicks than it does with dogs – and it should go without saying that dogs absolutely cannot eat chocolate Easter eggs.

1 April

Czech-French novelist Milan Kundera was born on this day in 1929. In his honour, today's dog is Karenin from his novel *The Unbearable Lightness of Being.*

> Karenin was not overjoyed by the move to Switzerland. Karenin hated change. Dog time cannot be plotted along a straight line; it does not move on and on, from one thing to the next. It moves in a circle like the hands of a clock, which – they, too, unwilling to dash madly ahead – turn round and round the face, day in and day out following the same path. In Prague, when Tomas and Tereza bought a new chair or moved a flower pot, Karenin would look on in displeasure. It was as though they were trying to dupe the hands of the clock by changing the numbers on its face.

2 April

English writer Sue Townsend was born on this day in 1946. To mark the occasion, today's dog is the unnamed family pet from her beloved 1982 book *The Secret Diary of Adrian Mole, Aged 13¾.*

> The dog has got the same colour eyes as Pandora. I only noticed because my mother cut the dog's hair. It looks worse than ever. Mr Lucas and my mother were laughing at the dog's new haircut, which is not very nice, because dogs can't answer back, just like the Royal Family.

3 April

American writer Washington Irving was born on this day in 1783. Our dog today is Wolf, who features in Irving's popular short story 'Rip Van Winkle'. At the story's opening, Rip Van Winkle is a Dutch-American man given to idleness, something that infuriates his wife – and she sometimes blames Wolf for her husband's lazy attitude.

> Rip's sole domestic adherent was his dog Wolf, who was as much hen-pecked as his master; for Dame Van Winkle regarded them as companions in idleness, and even looked upon Wolf with an evil eye, as the cause of his master's going so often astray. True it is, in all points of spirit befitting an honourable dog, he was as courageous an animal as ever scoured the woods; but what courage can withstand the ever-during and all-besetting terrors of a woman's tongue? The moment Wolf entered the house his crest fell, his tail drooped to the ground, or curled beneath his legs, he sneaked about with a gallows air, casting many a sidelong glance at Dame Van Sinkle, and at the least flourish of a broomstick or ladle he would fly to the door with yelping precipitation.

4 April

French writer Antoine de Saint-Exupéry's beautiful novella *The Little Prince* was published in April 1943, and has touched and delighted readers ever since. Among the many wonderful characters the little prince encounters is a wise fox.

'For me you're only a little boy just like a hundred thousand other little boys. And I have no need of you. And you have no need of me, either. For you I'm only a fox like a hundred thousand other foxes. But if you tame me, we'll need each other. You'll be the only boy in the world – for me. I'll be the only fox in the world for you.'

5 April

Today's dog is Sergeant Murphy, the police officer pooch featured in Richard Scarry's beloved *Busytown* children's books. With his positive, can-do attitude and smart uniform, Sergeant Murphy spends his days riding around on his motorcycle, directing traffic and dealing with reassuringly low-stakes scenarios.

6 April

So there we were, alone together. Jack was a mongrel, or mixed breed as they say now. He was rough-haired and had a strong little body and a pointed, foxy face which at the same time expressed a willingness towards the human which you would never find in a fox.

He took to me. I let him sniff my hand and I fed him and made him walk behind me through doorways – Nora had told me this was important – and we began to go for long walks together.

– Helen Dunmore, *Birdcage Walk*

7 April

English Romantic poet William Wordsworth was born on this day in 1770. To mark the day, enjoy these lines from his poem 'Tribute to the Memory of the Same Dog'.

We grieved for thee, and wished thy end were past;
And willingly have laid thee here at last:
For thou hadst lived till everything that cheers
In thee had yielded to the weight of years;
Extreme old age had wasted thee away,
And left thee but a glimmering of the day;
Thy ears were deaf, and feeble were thy knees,—
I saw thee stagger in the summer breeze,
Too weak to stand against its sportive breath,
And ready for the gentlest stroke of death.
[...] For love, that comes wherever life and sense
Are given by God, in thee was most intense;
A chain of heart, a feeling of the mind,
A tender sympathy, which did thee bind
Not only to us Men, but to thy Kind:
Yea, for thy fellow-brutes in thee we saw
A soul of love, love's intellectual law.

8 April

English horror writer James Herbert was born on this day in 1943. Today's dog is the eponymous hero of his novel *Fluke*, a dog who realizes that he used to be a man, and tries to work out how he ended up in canine form.

> For me, it was to be different. The memories might still linger, to surface occasionally, but the emotions had changed. My emotions were fast becoming those of a dog, as though, now my search was over, a ghost had been vanquished. The ghost was my humanness. I felt free, free as any bird in the sky. Free to live as a dog. I ran for nearly a day and, when I finally dropped, the last remnants of my old self had been purged.

9 April

French poet and essayist Charles Baudelaire was born on this day in 1821. His collection of prose poems, *Le Spleen de Paris*, was published posthumously in 1869, and includes a piece titled '*Le Chien et le Flacon*', or 'The Dog and the Vial'. This describes the way that a dog will react with horror if offered a vial of perfume to sniff, but will delightedly snuffle every possible scent out of a pile of excrement.

> 'My pretty dog, my good dog, my doggy dear, come and smell this excellent perfume bought at the best scent-shop in the city.'

And the dog, wagging its tail, which is, I think, the poor creature's substitute for a laugh or a smile, approached and curiously placed its damp nose to the opened vial; then, recoiling with sudden fright, it growled at me in reproach.

10 April

A dog don't cheat, a dog don't lie. Dogs remind you of you: they give everything they've got, they're wide open to the world.

– Zadie Smith, 'Crazy They Call Me'

11 April

Today's dogs are the hunting hounds of Actaeon in Greek mythology. In most versions of the story, Actaeon is out hunting in the woods when he comes across the goddess Artemis bathing. He stares at her naked body, and in revenge Artemis transforms him into a stag. His pack of hunting dogs, no longer able to recognize their master, give chase, and ultimately tear him to shreds.

12 April

On this day in 1951, American writer E B White, author of *Charlotte's Web* and *Stuart Little*, wrote a scathing yet hilarious letter to the American Society for the Prevention of Cruelty to Animals after being accused of not paying tax on his dog Minnie.

> You asked about Minnie's name, sex, breed and phone number. She doesn't answer the phone. She is a dachshund and can't reach it, but she wouldn't answer it even if she could, as she has no interest in outside calls.

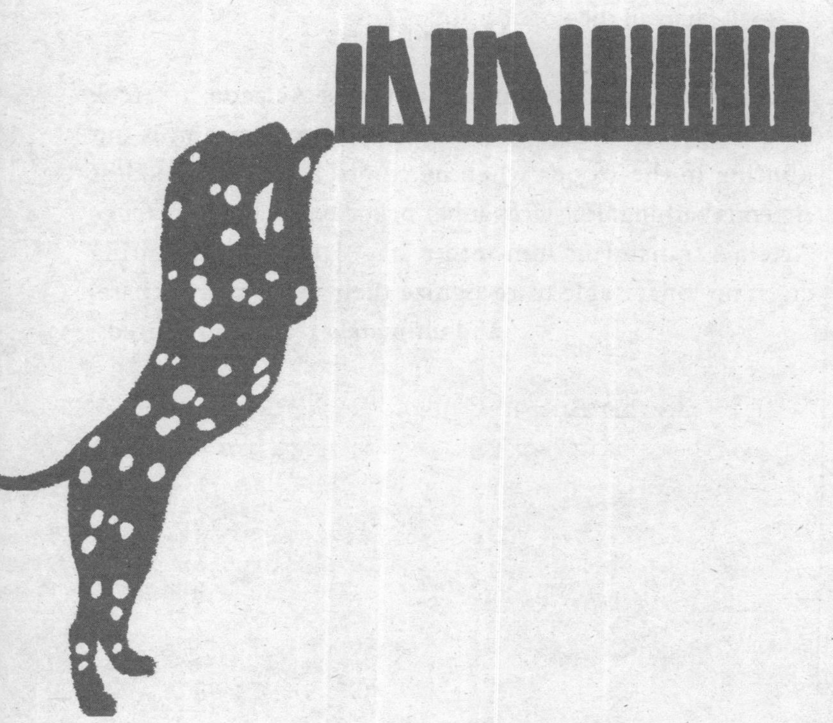

13 April

Irish playwright and poet Samuel Beckett was born on this day in 1906. His mother, May Beckett, kept Kerry Blue terriers, and Samuel was particularly fond of one named Wolf. Although she is our dog of the day, let's hope the quote below, spoken by Vladimir in Beckett's iconic play *Waiting for Godot*, has nothing to do with her.

> A dog came in the kitchen
> And stole a crust of bread.
> Then cook up with a ladle
> And beat him till he was dead.
>
> […] Then all the dogs came running
> And dug the dog a tomb
> And wrote upon the tombstone
> For the eyes of dogs to come:
>
> A dog came in the kitchen …

14 April

We'll be meeting British writer J R Ackerley properly on 4 November, but for now please enjoy these words, spoken by a wise vet in his book *My Dog Tulip*.

> Dogs aren't difficult to understand. One has to put oneself in their position.

15 April

The Turn of the Screw author Henry James was born on this day in 1843. He had a dachshund called Max, whom he described in a letter of August 1904.

> Lastly, I take the liberty of confiding to your charity and humanity the precious little person of my Dachshund Max, who is the best and gentlest and most reasonable and well-mannered as well as most beautiful, small animal of his kind to be easily come across – so that I think you will speedily find yourselves loving him for his own sweet sake. [...] Of course what he most intensely dreams of is being taken out on walks, and the more you are able to indulge him the more he will adore you and the more all the latent beauty of his nature will come out.

16 April

Our dog today is Bello, the Great Dane featured in Meindert DeJong's 1939 children's book *Dirk's Dog, Bello.* The book is set in a small Dutch fishing village, and sees a young boy named Dirk rescue a dog from a shipwreck. The two soon become fast friends, but keeping – and feeding – a dog of Bello's size is a challenge. Below is a song Dirk sings about his four-legged companion.

> Have you ever seen such a gigantic Dog?
> He eats cow legs and baby sharks,
> And his name is Bello, the Dane.

17 April

Colombian writer Gabriel García Márquez died on this day in 2014. His short story 'Eyes of a Blue Dog' depicts a man and a woman who keep meeting in their dreams, and agree upon a phrase to use to try and find one another in the waking world.

> She said that she went into restaurants and before ordering said to the waiter, 'Eyes of a blue dog.' But the waiters bowed reverently, without remembering ever having said that in their dreams. Then she would write on the napkins and scratch on the varnish of the tables with a knife, 'Eyes of a blue dog.' And on the steamed-up windows of hotels, stations, all public buildings she would write with her forefinger, 'Eyes of a blue dog.'

18 April

Today's dog is Bouboule (later renamed Piccolo), the poodle pal of diarist and author Anaïs Nin. Nin's lover, Rupert Pole, had a dog of his own named Tavi, and the pair often wrote to each other about their respective hounds. The extract below comes from an undated letter Nin sent to Pole from Paris.

> Bouboule is getting some education. He is a fine audience – never coughs or barks – bows to applauses – and what a job to keep him clean in the rainy Paris. Dogs have to wear booties! I finally had to get him some. As long as it is pretty (just like me) he'll wear it! I had to put a piece of plastic under his red coat. He comes in looking like Tavi after a swim!

19 April

Lord Byron died on this day in 1824. We've already learned about his deep love for his dog Boatswain (22 January), but legend has it that when he attended Trinity College, Cambridge, the young Lord Byron was so enraged by the college's 'no dogs allowed' rule that he brought a bear with him instead. Apparently the college hadn't thought to ban those of the ursine persuasion. He is even said to have tried to enrol the bear as a student.

20 April

Our dog today comes to us from the wonderful world of Greek mythology – specifically the Underworld. Cerberus is the fearsome many-headed hound said to guard the gates to Hades. Although he is often depicted as having three heads (and that's certainly the figure Dante goes for in his *Inferno*), other tellings give him fifty or even a hundred. Cerberus's most famous outing in mythology is when he is captured by Heracles as part of his Twelve Labours, although he also appears in the story of Aeneas, where the terrifying guard dog is subdued with the help of some honey cakes that contain sleep-inducing herbs.

21 April

American writer Mark Twain died on this day in 1910. Our hound today comes from his 1904 short story 'A Dog's Tale'. Despite the delightful opening below, dog-lovers should proceed with caution if seeking out the rest of the story – it's not a happy one.

> My father was a St Bernard, my mother was a collie, but I am a Presbyterian. This is what my mother told me, I do not know these nice distinctions myself. To me they are only fine large words meaning nothing. My mother had a fondness for such; she liked to say them, and see other dogs look surprised and envious, as wondering how she got so much education. But, indeed, it was no

real education; it was only show: she got the words by listening in the dining-room and drawing-room when there was company, and by going with the children to Sunday-school and listening there; and whenever she heard a large word she said it over to herself many times, and so was able to keep it until there was a dogmatic gathering in the neighbourhood, then she would get it off, and surprise and distress them all, from pocket-pup to mastiff, which rewarded her for all her trouble.

22 April

'He howls mostly at night,' Cartwright said, 'but sometimes during the day. It's driving me crazy. I can't stand that continual howling. You know, a dog howls when there's a death due to occur in the neighbourhood.'

– Erle Stanley Gardner, *The Case of the Howling Dog*

23 April

Today marks the birthday of playwright and poet William Shakespeare. In his honour, today's dog is Crab from his play *The Two Gentlemen of Verona*. Crab's master, the fool Launce, frequently finds himself taking the blame for his dog's mischief in an effort to keep the pup from being punished. His speech below comes from Act IV, Scene IV.

When a man's servant shall play the cur with him, look you, it goes hard: one that I brought up of a puppy, one that I saved from drowning, when three or four of his blind brothers and sisters went to it! I have taught him – even as one would say precisely, Thus I would teach a dog. I was sent to deliver him as a present to Mistress Silvia from my master; and I came no sooner into the dining-chamber, but he steps me to her trencher, and steals her capon's leg. O, 'tis a foul thing when a cur cannot keep himself in all companies! I would have, as one should say, one that takes upon him to be a dog indeed, to be, as it were, a dog at all things. If I had not had more wit than he, to take a fault upon me that he did, I think verily he had been hang'd for it; sure as I live, he had suffer'd for it: you shall judge. He thrusts me himself into the company of three or four gentlemanlike dogs, under the Duke's table. He had not been there (bless the mark!) a pissing while, but all the chamber smelt him. *Out with the dog,* says one; *What cur is that?* says another. *Whip him out,* says the third; *Hang him up,* says the Duke. I, having been acquainted with the smell before, knew it was Crab; and goes me to the fellow that whips the dogs: *Friend,* quoth I, *you mean to whip the dog? Ay, marry, do I,* quoth he. *You do him the more wrong,* quoth I; *'twas I did the thing you wot of.* He makes me no more ado, but whips me out of the chamber. How many masters would do this for their servant. Nay, I'll be sworn, I have sat in the stocks for puddings he hath stol'n, otherwise he had been executed; I have stood on the pillory for geese he hath kill'd, otherwise he had suffer'd for't.

24 April

English novelist Anthony Trollope was born on this day in 1815. Today's dog is not strictly a dog at all, but rather the name of the pub at the heart of his short story 'The Spotted Dog'.

> We went in and out of the Spotted Dog as if we had known that establishment all our lives, and spent many a quarter of an hour with the hostess in her little parlour, discussing the prospect of Mr Mackenzie and his family.

25 April

Daniel Defoe's classic adventure novel *Robinson Crusoe* was first published on this day in 1719. During his long years stranded on the deserted island, Crusoe enjoys the company of two cats and a dog – although it has to be said that, considering his very limited number of companions, he doesn't actually mention the dog all that often.

> And I must not forget, that we had in the ship a dog, and two cats [...] I carried both the cats with me; and as for the dog, he jumped out of the ship of himself, and swam on shore to me the day after I went on shore with my first cargo, and was a trusty servant to me many years; I wanted nothing that he could fetch me, nor any company that he could make up to me; I only wanted to have him talk to me, but that would not do.

26 April

Today's dog is Winn-Dixie, the loveable pooch at the heart of Kate DiCamillo's 2000 children's novel *Because of Winn-Dixie*. It tells the story of Opal, who encounters a stray dog in a supermarket, and pretends that he is hers to save him from the pound. Winn-Dixie's friendly nature draws people to him, and so helps Opal get to know the community around her.

> Once we were safe outside, I checked him over real careful and he didn't look that good. He was big but skinny; you could see his ribs. And there were bald patches all over him, places where he didn't have any fur at all. Mostly, he looked like a big piece of old brown carpet that had been left out in the rain.
>
> 'You're a mess,' I told him. 'I bet you don't belong to anybody.'
>
> He smiled at me. He did that thing again, where he pulled back his lips and showed me his teeth. He smiled so big that it made him sneeze. It was like he was saying, 'I know I'm a mess. Isn't it funny?'
>
> It's hard not to immediately fall in love with a dog who has a good sense of humour.

27 April

Austrian-American writer Ludwig Bemelmans was born on this day in 1898. He is best known for writing and illustrating the delightful *Madeline* books, describing a boarding school in Paris where there lived 'twelve little girls / in two straight lines'. Today's dog is Madeline's pet Genevieve, who first appears after rescuing Madeline when she falls into the River Seine.

> The dog loves biscuits, milk and beef
> And they named it Genevieve.
> She could sing and almost talk
> And enjoyed the daily walk.

28 April

Beloved English author Terry Pratchett was born on this day in 1948. To celebrate, today's dog is Gaspode, a wiry-haired talking pooch who features in a number of Pratchett's *Discworld* novels including *Men at Arms* and *Moving Pictures*.

> It was true that normal people couldn't hear Gaspode speak, because dogs *don't* speak. It's a well-known fact. It's well known at the organic level, like a lot of other well-known facts which overrule the observations of the senses. This is because if people went around noticing everything that was going on all time, no one would ever get anything done. Besides, almost all dogs don't talk. Ones that do are merely a statistical error, and can therefore be ignored.

29 April

Today's dog is Cyril, the delightfully self-assured bulldog who appears in Connie Willis's 1997 unpredictable, time-travelling comedy *To Say Nothing of the Dog.*

Cyril had staked out his claim and refused to move.

'Move over!' I said, freeing one hand from holding the cat to push. 'Dogs are supposed to sleep at the foot of the bed.'

Cyril had never heard of this rule. He jammed his body up against my back and began to snore.

30 April

When the man had finished [eating], he filled his pipe and took his comfortable time over a smoke. Then he pulled on his mittens, settled the ear flaps of his cap firmly about his ears, and took the creek trail up the left fork. The dog was disappointed and yearned back toward the fire. This man did not know cold. Possibly all the generations of his ancestry had been ignorant of cold, of real cold, of cold one hundred and seven degrees below freezing point. But the dog knew; all its ancestry knew, and it had inherited the knowledge. And it knew that it was not a good time to walk abroad in such fearful cold. It was the time to lie snug in a hole in the snow and wait for a curtain of cloud to be drawn across the face of outer space whence this cold came.

– Jack London, 'To Build a Fire'

MAY

Summer is fast approaching, and the longer days and warm weather mean it's the perfect time to hit the great outdoors and enjoy some good long walks. This month's dogs are faithful, brave and wise – we have one who can read (8 May), one who can talk (18 May) and one who can, apparently, understand Greek (20 May).

May is Mental Health Awareness Month – and, as any dog-lover knows, there is no greater balm on difficult days than sharing space with a gentle pooch. See 6 May for just some of the things we can learn from dogs about finding peace and joy in the every day.

Moveable feasts

MOTHER'S DAY (US): See 'Moveable Feasts' in March.

1 May

Mark Haddon's hit novel *The Curious Incident of the Dog in the Night-Time* was published on this day in 2003. Today's dog is Wellington, the poor poodle whose murder is at the crux of this story.

> Wellington was a poodle. Not one of the small poodles that have hairstyles but a big poodle. It had curly black fur, but when you got close you could see that the skin underneath the fur was a very pale yellow, like chicken.
>
> I stroked Wellington and wondered who had killed him and why.

2 May

English writer Jerome K Jerome was born on this day in 1859. He is best known for his comedy travelogue *Three Men in a Boat (To Say Nothing of the Dog)* – which, incidentally, inspired the name and part of the story for the book we discussed on 29 April. Today's dog is Montmorency, the pooch who joins the three men on their boating trip along the Thames.

> [Montmorency] does not revel in romantic solitude. Give him something noisy; and if a trifle low, so much the jollier. To look at Montmorency you would imagine that he was an angel sent upon the earth, for some reason withheld from mankind, in the shape of a small fox-terrier. There is a sort of Oh-what-a-wicked-world-this-is-and-how-I-wish-I-could-do-something-to-make-

it-better-and-nobler expression about Montmorency that has been known to bring the tears into the eyes of pious old ladies and gentlemen.

[...] To hang about a stable, and collect a gang of the most disreputable dogs to be found in the town, and lead them out to march round the slums to fight other disreputable dogs, is Montmorency's idea of 'life', and so, as I before observed, he gave to the suggestion of inns, and pubs, and hotels his most emphatic approbation.

3 May

English writer Dodie Smith was born on this day in 1896. We've already met the stars of her famous story *The Hundred and One Dalmatians* (14 February and Mother's Day in March), but today let's enjoy some wise words on language and communication from that same book.

Dogs can never speak the language of humans and humans can never speak the language of dogs. But many dogs can understand almost every word humans say, while humans seldom learn to recognise more than half a dozen barks, if that. And barks are only a small part of the dog language. A wagging tail can mean so many things. Humans know that it means a dog is pleased, but not what the dog is saying about its pleasedness. (Really, it is very clever of humans to understand a wagging tail at all, as they have no tails of their own.) Then there are the snufflings and sniffings, the pricking of ears – all meaning different things. And many, many words are expressed by a dog's eyes.

4 May

In Rachel Yoder's 2021 novel *Nightbitch,* a young mother who spends day after day at home alone with her toddler starts to experience strange cravings and physical changes – including the growth of new patches of hair, sharper teeth ... and a tail.

> On Monday morning, she did what any totally and completely normal person would do who had recently transformed into a dog and sat on the toilet with the lid down, searching the internet as she listened to her husband and son move about the house. She started with *werewolf facts* and *real monsters,* then moved on to *shapeshifting* and *shapeshifting Native American,* then *skinwalkers* and *Navajo witches.* She read and read, but what she wanted to find was a mother who turned into a dog – a regular domesticated dog capable of being a pet – and so she kept on.

5 May

German philosopher, writer and revolutionary socialist Karl Marx was born on this day in 1818. His family home was filled with pets, including cats, birds and dogs. When his daughter Eleanor was away visiting her older sister in 1869, Marx wrote to her to tell her how much her dog Whiskey missed her:

> Whiskey, this big and good personality, was at first, like Calipso, not to be consoled and was in despair over your trip. He refused the best bones, never left the bedroom, evinced throughout all the symptoms of deep sorrow of a *schöne Seele* [beautiful soul].

6 May

> A person can learn a lot from a dog, even a loopy one like ours. [...] Marley taught me about living each day with unbridled exuberance and joy, about seizing the moment and following your heart. He taught me to appreciate the simple things – a walk in the woods, a fresh snowfall, a nap in a shaft of winter sunlight. And as he grew old and achy, he taught me about optimism in the face of adversity. Mostly, he taught me about friendship and selflessness and, above all else, unwavering loyalty.
>
> – John Grogan, *Marley and Me*

7 May

English writer Angela Carter was born on this day in 1940. What better way to mark the day than with an extract from her stunning short story 'The Company of Wolves', which appeared in her seminal collection *The Bloody Chamber*.

One beast and only one howls in the woods by night.

The wolf is carnivore incarnate and he's as cunning as he is ferocious; once he's had a taste of flesh then nothing else will do.

At night, the eyes of wolves shine like candle flames, yellowish, reddish […] If the benighted traveller spies those luminous, terrible sequins stitched suddenly on the black thickets, then he knows he must run, if fear has not struck him stock-still.

8 May

American novelist Thomas Pynchon was born on this day in 1937. Today's dog is Pugnax, who appears in his hefty 2006 novel *Against the Day*. Pugnax is an honorary member of an airship crew known as the Chums of Chance – oh, and he can read.

At one end of the gondola, largely oblivious to the coming and going on deck, with his tail thumping expressively now and then against the planking, and his nose among the pages of a volume by Mr Henry James, lay a dog of no particular breed, to all appearances absorbed by the text before him.

9 May

We met poet Alexander Pope and the fictional Shock back on 21 March, but today's dog is of the real-life variety: Pope's own beloved pet, Bounce, a Great Dane. When Bounce gave birth to a litter of puppies, Pope presented one of them to Frederick, Prince of Wales, with the following epigram engraved on its collar:

> I am his highness' dog at Kew;
> Pray tell me, Sir, whose dog are you?

10 May

English writer Richard Adams was born on this day in 1920. Best known for *Watership Down*, his tale about a group of rabbits searching for a new home, he also wrote *The Plague Dogs*, which tells the story of a pair of dogs, Rowf and Snitter, who escape from a government testing facility where they have been subjected to brutal experiments. They go on the run and, with the help of a fox known as The Tod, the two dogs learn to survive as they try to evade their pursuers.

> 'We've tried your way, Snitter. Now we'll try mine. That mouse isn't the only one who can do without men. We can *change* if we want to. Do you know that? *Change* – into wild animals!'
>
> He flung up his head and howled to the blotted-out, invisible sky. 'Damn men! Damn all men! Change! Change!'

11 May

Scottish author Sheila Burnford was born on this day in 1916. Her novel *The Incredible Journey* tells the story of two dogs and a cat travelling through the Canadian wilderness after becoming separated from their owners. Today's dogs, then, are Luath and Bodger, who along with the cat Tao must try to survive the wild and return home to their humans. Luath, a young Labrador retriever, often leads the way, but it is the old and tired bull terrier Bodger who most often captures readers' hearts.

12 May

English artist and writer Edward Lear was born on this day in 1812. He was famous for his nonsense poetry, including this delightful dog-related limerick.

There was a Young Lady of Ryde,
whose shoe-strings were seldom untied;
She purchased some clogs,
and some small spotty dogs,
And frequently walked about Ryde.

13 May

Today's dog is Rab, the eponymous hero of the 1859 short story 'Rab and His Friends', written by Scottish writer Dr John Brown. Rab is a fierce but deeply loyal mastiff whom the story's narrator first encounters fighting off an attack from another dog in the street. As he grows up, the narrator gets to know Rab, and learns how completely devoted he is to his master, the carter James Noble.

> Rab I saw almost every week, on the Wednesday; and we had much pleasant intimacy. I found the way to his heart by frequent scratching of his huge head, and an occasional bone. When I did not notice him he would plant himself straight before me, and stand wagging that bud of a tail, and looking up, with his head a little to the one side.

14 May

> [T]he [only] exception I make to my rigid antischmaltz policy is for dogs. At the heart of that exception was Rex. In his presence, my normally dry, undemonstrative personality flipped upside down. I talked baby talk to him. I hugged him constantly. I told him I loved him approximately eighteen times a day. I used words like *furrylicious.* I entered him in a charity 'mutt show' contest in the category of 'best coat' and was incensed for weeks afterward (in truth: months, possibly years) when he didn't win.
>
> – Meghan Daum, 'The Dog Exception'

15 MAY

Today's dog comes from the fairy tale 'The Dog and the Sparrow' by the Brothers Grimm. It features a poor hungry sheepdog who has run away from his owner after being badly treated. The dog encounters a sparrow and shares his plight, and the sparrow kindly gathers food for his new friend. Sadly, being a Grimms' fairy tale, all does not end happily. While sleeping, the dog is crushed by a wagon – and the furious sparrow swears revenge on the wagon's driver.

> [T]he sparrow cried, 'Thou hast killed the dog my brother, and it shall cost thee horses and cart!'
>
> 'Oh! horses and cart!' said the waggoner, 'what harm can you do me, I should like to know?' and drove on.

Famous last words. The waggoner ends up losing not only his horses and cart, but also his crop – and his life.

16 MAY

On this day in 1937, writer and dog-lover Edith Wharton wrote a letter to her friend William R Tyler lamenting the death of her precious Pekinese, Linky – and sharing with him that she had always felt able to communicate with the little creature.

> I lost two *very* old friends within a few days of each other – my little Linky, and then dear Lady Wemyss, who has been here with me so lately. It would seem odd to most

people that I should group them together, but *you* will know and understand.

During the last years of the Roman Empire the Emperors had a passion for human 'curiosities', such as mermaids, fauns, centaurs, etc.— There were professional collectors, and whenever one was found, he, she, or it was shipped to Rome. [...] Once they found a boy who *understood what the birds said*; and I have always been like that about dogs, ever since I was a baby. We really communicated with each other – and no one had such wise things to say as Linky ...

17 May

Before Ariana, before Cynthia, even before Judy Garland, there was L Frank Baum's novel *The Wonderful Wizard of Oz,* in which readers first met the characters that have since become cultural icons. Today's dog is, of course, Toto.

It was Toto that made Dorothy laugh, and saved her from growing as grey as her surroundings. Toto was not grey; he was a little black dog, with long silky hair and small black eyes that twinkled merrily on either side of his funny wee nose. Toto played all day long, and Dorothy played with him, and loved him dearly.

18 May

Today's dog is Molly, who appears in *John Dies at the End*, a horror-comedy novel written by David Wong (a pseudonym used by American author Jason Pargin). Molly – whom the narrator Dave describes as 'maybe an Irish setter or a red Labrador or a ... Scottish rustdog' – seems to 'choose' Dave as her new owner when he attends a party. As the story develops, things start getting very strange, and Molly begins 'speaking' in the voice of David's friend John, from whom he has been separated. Although John can speak to David through Molly, it turns out Molly is still in there, and her dog nature tends to interrupt their conversations.

> A filthy grey cat zipped across the trailer park, across the front of the car and off into the distance. Molly pulled her head inside and tromped over to the driver's-side window, stomping on my crotch and shouting 'CAT!!!' the whole way. It took ten minutes to get the dog calmed down, at which point she promptly curled up and went to sleep in the passenger seat.
>
> 'John?'
>
> The dog farted. I got nothing else out of her the rest of the night.

19 May

American writer, journalist and filmmaker Nora Ephron was born on this day in 1941. Here are some wise words she shared on dealing with an empty nest in her essay collection *I Feel Bad About My Neck.*

> If you find yourself nostalgic for the ongoing, day-to-day activities required of the modern parent, there's a solution: get a dog. I don't recommend it, because dogs require tremendous commitment, but they definitely give you something to do. Plus they're very loveable and, more important, uncritical. And they can be trained.

20 May

We first encountered Flush, canine companion to Elizabeth Barrett Browning, on 6 March. There we saw him through the eyes of Virginia Woolf. Here, we learn about him in a letter written by his mistress in 1842.

> You understand – don't you? – that Flush is my constant companion, my friend, my amusement, lying with his head on one of my folios while I read the other. (Not *your* folios – I respect your books, to be sure.) Oh, I dare say, if the truth were know, Flush understands Greek excellently well.

21 May

Charlotte Perkins Gilman's 1915 novel *Herland* imagines a feminist utopia made up entirely of women, and depicts a group of three men who form an expedition to seek out this strange society. When they encounter the inhabitants of Herland, the characters engage in lengthy discussions about the differences between their societies – and it turns out that the women of Herland find the idea of keeping dogs very strange, preferring to enjoy the company of cats.

> 'Are all these breeds of dog you have made useful?' they asked.
>
> 'Oh – useful! Why, the hunting dogs and watchdogs and sheepdogs are useful – and sled dogs of course! – and ratters, I suppose, but we don't keep dogs for their *usefulness.* The dog is "the friend of man", we say – we love them.'
>
> That they understood. 'We love our cats that way. They surely are our friends, and helpers too. You can see how intelligent and affectionate they are.'

22 May

Belgian cartoonist Hergé, aka Georges Prosper Remi, was born on this day in 1907. His series *The Adventures of Tintin* is one of the best-known comics of all time, and introduced readers to Snowy, Tintin's white terrier. Snowy is brave, loyal and resourceful. In the very first Tintin story, 1929's *Tintin in the Land of the Soviets,* we see Snowy use a banana skin to foil an enemy's plan to injure his master.

23 May

Stephen King's 1978 novel *The Stand* describes a world torn apart by a deadly pandemic, with the ravaged population forced to travel far and wide in order to try and find fellow survivors. Our dog today is Kojak (formerly Big Steve), an Irish setter who joins the group of mismatched travellers at the centre of *The Stand.* At one stage, the group make the devastating decision to leave Kojak behind as they plan to travel by motorcycle. Later in the novel, the brave and loyal dog shows up again, having painstakingly tracked the group across the country, fighting off wolves and struggling to survive in order to be reunited with his humans.

> Kojak was lying on the porch, his tattered snout laid peacefully on his forepaws. The dog was rack-thin and pitifully chewed, but Stu recognised him, even on short acquaintance. He squatted and began to stroke Kojak's head. Kojak woke up and looked happily at Stu. In the way that dogs have, he seemed to grin.
>
> 'Say, that's a good dog,' Stu said, feeling a lump in his throat [...]. 'Good dog,' he repeated, and Kojak thumped his tail against the porch boards, presumably agreeing that he was, indeed a good dog.

24 May

Today's dog is Pickles, a terrier who co-owns a shop with a yellow tomcat in Beatrix Potter's *The Tale of Ginger and Pickles.* The two work together to serve their customers, with

Pickles serving the mice so that Ginger won't be tempted to devour them, and Ginger returning the favour with the rats. As Pickles solemnly acknowledges: 'It would never do to eat our own customers; they would leave us and go to Tabitha Twitchit's.' Despite managing to avoid consuming their clientele, Ginger and Pickles make the mistake of allowing all their customers unlimited credit, and are eventually forced to close the shop as they run out of money.

25 May

Day after day, the whole day through—
Wherever my road inclined—
Four-Feet said, 'I am coming with you!'
And trotted along behind.

– Rudyard Kipling, 'Four-Feet'

26 May

Bram Stoker's seminal vampire novel *Dracula* was first published on this day in 1897. Here we see the chilling moment when the ship the *Demeter*, which had been transporting Count Dracula along with boxes of earth from his home, runs aground at Whitby. The *Demeter* seems to be a ghost ship, with no crew left aboard, and the corpse of a man lashed to the helm. The only sign of life is a huge hound that leaps ashore as the ship arrives.

> But, strangest of all, the very instant the shore was touched, an immense dog sprang up on deck from below, as if shot up by the concussion, and running forward, jumped from the bow on the sand. Making straight for the steep cliff, where the churchyard hangs over the laneway to the East Pier so steeply that some of the flat tombstones – 'thruff-steans' or 'through-stones', as they call them in the Whitby vernacular – actually project over where the sustaining cliff has fallen away, it disappeared into the darkness, which seemed intensified just beyond the focus of the searchlight.

27 May

On this day in 1936, American author John Steinbeck wrote to his editor with some bad news: his dog, Toby, had devoured part of an early draft of *Of Mice and Men*.

> Minor tragedy stalked. My setter pup, left alone one night, made confetti of about half of my book. Two months work to do over again. It sets me back. There was no other draft. [...] I was pretty mad but the poor little fellow may have been acting critically. [...] I'm not sure Toby didn't know what he was doing when he ate the first draft. I have promoted Toby-dog to be a lieutenant-colonel in charge of literature.

A small fragment of the original manuscript that survived the assault, measuring just 63 by 50mm, was sold at auction in 2023 for $12,800.

28 May

British writer Ian Fleming was born on this day in 1908. The *James Bond* author was famously pictured by photographer Harry Benson sitting in his study at his Goldeneye estate in Jamaica, hard at work, with two beautiful dogs looking on. Fleming biographer Matthew Parker has said that the 007 creator kept many dogs, including one named Fox – and a guard dog named Himmler.

29 May

British writer T H White, author of Arthurian fantasy novels including *The Sword in the Stone*, was born on this day in 1906. White's most constant companion was his beloved red setter, Brownie. He wrote about her frequently in his letters and journal, and was inconsolable when she died. He wrote to one friend:

> I stayed with the grave for a week, so that I could go out twice a day and say, 'Good girl: sleepy girl: go to sleep, Brownie.' It was a saying she understood. I said it steadily. I suppose the chance of consciousness persisting for a week is several million to one, but that was the kind of chance I had to provide for.

30 May

Today's dog is Mouse, four-pawed companion of hero Harry Dresden in Jim Butcher's fantasy series *The Dresden Files.*

A shaggy section of the kitchen floor hauled itself to its feet and came to meet me with a sheepish, sleepy shuffle. My dog, Mouse, had started off as a fuzzy little grey puppy that fit into my coat pocket. Now, almost a year later, I sometimes wished I'd sent my coat to the cleaners or something. Mouse had gone from fuzz ball to fuzz barge. You couldn't guess at a breed to look at him, but at least one of his parents must have been a woolly mammoth. The dog's shoulders came nearly to my waist, and the vet didn't think he was finished growing yet. That translated into an awful lot of beast for my tiny apartment.

31 May

The pine trees would look down forever on a lantern burning out of oil but not going out. A harvest moon would cast shadows forever of a man walking upright, his dog bouncing after him. And the quiet of the night would fill and echo again with the deep voice of Sounder, the great coon dog.

– William Armstrong, *Sounder*

JUNE

We've reached the year's midpoint, and summer is finally here. The best way to spend these bright, sunny days is to while away the hours in the garden or a park with a good book – better still if you have a canine pal to keep you company.

This month's distinguished dogs are magical (24 June), mythical (18 June) and medieval (15 June). We'll meet a boy who turns into a dog (5 June), and a dog who is (sort of) turned into a man (27 June).

Moveable feasts

FATHER'S DAY: Father's Day is usually celebrated on the third Sunday in June, and this month we pay tribute to two deeply devoted dog dads: Charles Dickens (9 June) and Anton Chekov (29 June).

1 June

Roald Dahl's magical children's book *Fantastic Mr Fox* was first published on this day in 1970. It tells the story of a wily fox who manages to outsmart a group of local farmers when they attempt to destroy his home before lying in wait for him with guns – a move that means all the animals who live underground, including the badgers, the moles and the rabbits, are trapped. Mr Fox comes up with a clever plan to burrow further underground and steal from underneath the farmers' noses, securing food for his family and friends, saving the day and generally being very dashing.

> Mr Fox grinned slyly, showing sharp white teeth. 'If I am not mistaken, my dear Badger,' he said, 'we are now underneath the farm which belongs to that nasty little pot-bellied [...] Bunce. We are, in fact, directly underneath the most *interesting part* of that farm.'

2 June

Today's dog is Apollo, the Great Dane at the centre of Sigrid Nunez's 2018 novel *The Friend*. When the narrator's close friend dies, the narrator reluctantly takes Apollo in – and ends up falling in love with him.

> Your whole house smells of dog, says someone who comes to visit. I say I'll take care of it. Which I do by never inviting that person to visit again.

3 June

George Orwell's short essay 'A Hanging' describes a prisoner being executed by hanging in Burma (as Myanmar was then known). The essay explores the horror of what it means to end a person's life in this way, and depicts in detail the moments immediately before the hanging, as the prisoner is brought out into the yard. The proceedings are briefly interrupted by the appearance of a dog, who blunders innocently into the midst of this sombre moment.

> A dreadful thing had happened – a dog, come goodness knows whence, had appeared in the yard. It came bounding among us with a loud volley of barks, and leapt round us wagging its whole body, wild with glee at finding so many human beings together. It was a large woolly dog, half Airedale, half pariah. For a moment it pranced round us, and then, before anyone could stop it, it had made a dash for the prisoner, and jumping up tried to lick his face. Everyone stood aghast, too taken aback even to grab at the dog.
>
> [...] The prisoner, in the grasp of the two warders, looked on incuriously, as though this was another formality of the hanging. It was several minutes before someone managed to catch the dog.

4 June

Sometimes a fox is a fox – and sometimes it's a metaphor. In Ted Hughes' poem 'The Thought-Fox', published in 1957 as part of his collection *The Hawk in the Rain*, the poet describes how, while sitting before a blank page, the image of a fox appears in the dark forest of his mind, representing the spark of inspiration.

> Cold, delicately as the dark snow
> A fox's nose touches twig, leaf.

5 June

Children's book author Allan Ahlberg (who often worked in partnership with his wife Janet Ahlberg) was born on this day in 1938. His 1986 book *Woof!* tells the story of a boy called Eric Banks, who has an unusual secret – every now and then, he turns into a dog (a Norfolk terrier, to be precise).

> The time it took Eric to turn into a dog – his shape blurring and rippling like a swimmer under water – was about fifteen seconds. The time it took him to become frantic was about five seconds after that. His first action was to begin scrabbling in the bed, trying to get a better look at himself. His thoughts were in a turmoil: 'I'm a dog! A *dog!*' The next thing he did was to try to get out of bed. This wasn't easy for a dog in pyjamas; besides, they were baggy on him now. [...] He resisted the urge to growl when one of his claws got stuck in a buttonhole. He sat on the floor and thought: 'I'm a dog!'

6 June

Seamus Heaney's poem 'A Dog Was Crying To-night in Wicklow Also', dedicated to critic and academic Donatus Nwoga, reimagines an Igbo folktale in which a dog is tasked with delivering a message from the humans to the deity Chukwu, requesting that death be made temporary. Sadly, the dog is distracted from his task, and a toad ends up delivering the message instead – incorrectly.

> But death and human beings took second place
> When he trotted off the path and started barking
> At another dog in broad daylight just barking
> Back at him from the far bank of a river.

7 June

For it is by muteness that a dog becomes for one so utterly beyond value; with him one is at peace, where words play no torturing tricks. When he just sits, loving, and knows that he is being loved, those are the moments that I think are precious to a dog; when, with his adoring soul coming through his eyes, he feels that you are really thinking of him.

– John Galsworthy, *Memories*

8 June

Today's dog is Rollo, who appears in Diana Gabaldon's *Outlander* series. At his first appearance, when Young Ian wins him in a game of dice, the boy's aunt and uncle (the narrator, Claire, and her husband Jamie), mistake Rollo for a wolf. It turns out he is only *half* wolf, being the product of a liaison between a wolf and an Irish wolfhound. Whatever he is, he's big.

> 'See? It's a dog,' said Ian proudly.
>
> I took a quick half-step behind Jamie, grabbing his arm.
>
> 'Ian,' I said, 'that is not a dog. It's a wolf. It's a bloody *big* wolf, and I think you ought to get away from it before it takes a bite out of your arse.'
>
> The wolf twitched one ear negligently in my direction, dismissed me, and twitched it back. It continued to sit, panting with the heat, its big yellow eyes fixed on Ian with an intensity that might have been taken for devotion by someone who hadn't met a wolf before.

9 June

Charles Dickens died on this day in 1870. In a letter from March 1842, Dickens wrote:

> I went *incog.* behind the scenes to the little theatre where Mitchell is making a fortune. He has been rearing a little dog for me, and has called him 'Boz'. I am going to bring him home.

The dog in question, a white Havanese, did indeed go home with Dickens – although his name was changed. While 'Boz' was a very on-brand name, being Dickens's pen name, he opted to rename the pooch after an incidental character in *Nicholas Nickleby*. And so Boz became Mr Snittle Timbery – or Timber for short. He lived to an old age and accompanied Dickens on his travels across Europe.

10 June

Scottish author M C Beaton (real name Marion Gibbons) was born on this day in 1936. One of her best-known creations is the Highland police officer Hamish Macbeth, about whom she wrote dozens of books. Today's dog is Hamish's companion Towser, a sweet-natured and thoroughly spoilt pooch who prefers human food to dog food.

> 'You spoil that dog,' said Miss Gunnery as Hamish placed a fish supper on its cardboard tray down in front of Towser.
>
> Hamish did not reply. He knew he spoilt Towser but did not like anyone to comment on the fact.

11 June

American novelist William Styron was born on this day in 1925. Today's dog is his pet Aquinnah, a Labrador/golden retriever cross whose role as his walking companion was described by Styron in his essay 'Walking with Aquinnah'.

> One's dog – whose physiology prevents it from being a chatterbox – can be a wonderful companion [while walking], making no conversational demands while providing an animated connection with one's surroundings.

12 June

Frances Hodgson Burnett's 1905 children's novel *A Little Princess* tells the story of Sara Crewe, a young girl from a wealthy background who is sent to an elite boarding school while her father works abroad. Sara is nicknamed 'princess' due to the preferential treatment she is shown by the school's staff, but vows to always behave as kindly and bravely as she feels a princess would. After her father's financial ruin and sudden death, Sara is made to work as a maid by the school's headmistress, and is treated cruelly for years – until she is rescued by one Mr Carrisford, her father's former business partner, who is very wealthy and delights in buying Sara gifts, including one particularly special present.

She found beautiful new flowers growing in her room, whimsical little gifts tucked under her pillows, and once, as they sat together in the evening, they heard the scratch of a heavy paw on the door, and when Sara went to find out what it was, there stood a great dog – a splendid Russian boarhound – with a grand silver and gold collar bearing an inscription in raised letters. 'I am Boris,' it read; 'I serve the Princess Sara.'

13 June

English crime novelist Dorothy L Sayers was born on this day in 1893. Today's dog is the young hunting pup who makes a brief but ever so charming appearance in her first novel, *Whose Body?*.

Tuesday saw Lord Peter and a man in a velveteen jacket swishing merrily through seven acres of turnip-tops, streaked yellow with early frosts. A little way ahead, a sinuous undercurrent of excitement among the leaves proclaimed the unseen yet ever-near presence of one of the Duke of Denver's setter pups. Presently a partridge flew up with a noise like a police rattle, and Lord Peter accounted for it [...]. The setter bounded foolishly through the turnips, and fetched back the dead bird.

'Good dog,' said Lord Peter.

Encouraged by this, the dog gave a sudden ridiculous gambol and barked, its ear tossed inside out over its head.

[...] 'Fool of a dog, that,' said the man in velveteen; 'can't keep quiet.'

14 June

Can a dog be twins?

– Patricia Lockwood, *No One is Talking About This*

15 June

Today's dogs are of the medieval variety: the greyhounds owned by the monk at the heart of Geoffrey Chaucer's *The Monk's Tale,* part of *The Canterbury Tales.* Despite being a man of faith, the monk is fond of hunting, and uses his 'grehoundes' to help him catch his quarry.

Therefore he was a prikasour [hard rider] aright;
Grehoundes he hadde, as swift as fowel in flight:
Of prikyng and huntyng for the hare
Was al his list, for no cost wolde he spare.

16 June

Today marks Bloomsday, the day when fans of James Joyce's *Ulysses* celebrate the book and often gather for readings. We've already met one of the novel's canine inhabitants, the rather fearsome Garryowen (13 January). Today's dog is Athos, the pet of protagonist Leopold Bloom's late father Rudolph – who also offers us a link back to the endlessly loyal Argos of Homer's *Odyssey* (15 January).

Mr Bloom is the one whose thoughts are most in keeping with the occasion. The dogs' home they pass reminds him of his dead father's dog Athos, a scion, perhaps of the longlived Argos stock. 'Poor old Athos. Be good to Athos, Leopold, is my last wish. Thy will be done. We obey them in the grave ... He took it to heart, pined away. Quiet brute. Old men's dogs usually are.'

17 June

Today's dog is Cedric, who appears in Michelle Paver's chilling ghost story *Thin Air*, set in the Himalayas. The book's narrator is part of a team of mountaineers attempting to summit Kangchenjunga – and Cedric is the sweet-natured hound who attaches himself to their exhibition.

I'm finding it a strain being with people all the time, so I often wander off with the dog. My pony trod on his paw in the last village, and when I jumped down to make sure it wasn't broken, he got the wrong idea and followed me. He's ridiculously shaggy, like a cross between a collie and a sheep, and he'll fetch anything I throw, as long as it isn't a stick. I call him Cedric, because he has a trick of cocking his head that reminds me of my cousin's husband.

18 June

Our canine today is the fearsome Fenrir of Norse mythology. Said to be the son of the trickster god Loki and a giantess, Fenrir is an enormous wolf with incredible strength. After learning that he was destined to do them harm, the gods attempted to bind him. After two failed attempts, they finally succeeded in binding Fenrir with an unbreakable chain – but not before he'd bitten off the hand of one of the gods, Týr. Fenrir was left bound to a boulder, with a sword in his mouth forcing his jaws open – and there he will stay until Ragnarök, when it is said that he will break free and run through the world with his mouth wide open, devouring everything in his path – including the great god Odin.

19 June

Writer Salman Rushdie was born on this day in 1947. In his honour, today's dog is Bear the dog from his novel *Luka and the Fire of Life* (you will be pleased to hear that the novel also features a bear called Dog).

> Bear the dog was a chocolate Labrador, and a gentle, friendly dog, though sometimes a bit excitable and nervous; he absolutely could not dance, having, as the saying goes, four left feet, but to make up for his clumsiness he possessed the gift of perfect pitch, so he could sing up a storm, howling out the melodies of the most popular songs of the day, and never going out of tune.

20 June

I love to write, and so I do it daily. Right now I am sitting in my library, in my big leather writing chair, and I am, yes, writing. My little dog Lily, a Westie, sprawls at my feet. 'Good dog, Lily,' I croon. But Lily is not a good dog. She is a very naughty dog, and chief among her misdeeds is a fondness for pens. Lily is a writer's dog, I joke. I settle in to write and Lily settles in to steal my pen. I move my hand across the page and, whenever I stop, Lily pounces. She grabs my pen and scampers off, only to emerge minutes later with a disembowelled pen and a jaunty black moustache.

– Julia Cameron, *Write for Life*

21 June

Today's dog is Kipper, star of the series of children's books written and illustrated by Mick Inkpen. He made his first appearance in 1989's *The Blue Balloon,* and starred in his own book two years later. Ever since, this little brown-and-white dog has delighted thousands of children with his sweet adventures and gentle ways, appearing in dozens of books and even his own TV series.

22 June

We've already met one of the Grimms' fairy-tale dogs (15 May), so today let's dig into the world of Danish writer Hans Christian Andersen and meet some of his canines, specifically the three enormous dogs that appear in his tale 'The Tinderbox'. It tells the story of a soldier who is asked by a witch to enter a hollow tree and retrieve a magical tinderbox for her. While he is in there, he comes across three chests, each one guarded by a dog – one with 'eyes as big as teacups', one with 'eyes as big as mill wheels' and one with 'eyes each as big as the Round Tower'. By following the witch's instructions, the soldier is able to open the chests, which contain copper, silver and gold, and help himself to their contents. He also retrieves the tinderbox, but elects to cut off the witch's head and keep the object for himself – which is lucky, because it turns out that by using the tinderbox, he can summon the enormous-eyed dogs and get them to do his bidding. He ends up marrying a princess – while the dogs look on.

> The wedding celebrations lasted for a week, and the dogs sat at the table too, making big eyes.

23 June

> That night [the puppy] jumped into my bed and stared at me, as if he were looking me over. Then, perhaps because he missed his mother in Missouri, he went to sleep in my arms. I was an only child, and he now was an only dog.

This was the first of our many days and years together. We named him Skipper for the lively way he walked, but he was always just Skip to me.

– Willie Morris, *My Dog Skip*

24 June

Today's dog is the Disreputable Dog from Garth Nix's fantasy novel *Lirael*, part of his *Old Kingdom* series. The novel's protagonist, Lirael, is a librarian who decides to try and create a companion in the form of a dog-shaped 'sending', a being created using Charter magic that typically lacks a solid form and is used to send messages. What she ends up making is something rather different.

In the instant of that blink, the globe disappeared, leaving behind a dog. Not a cute, cuddly Charter sending of a puppy, but a waist-high black and tan mongrel that seemed to be entirely real, including its impressive teeth.

[…] Suddenly, the dog […] stood up and shook itself, spraying droplets of water all over Lirael and all over the study. Then it ambled across and licked the petrified girl on the face with a tongue that most definitely was all real dog and not some Charter-made imitation.

When that got no response, it grinned and announced, 'I am the Disreputable Dog. Or Disreputable Bitch, if you want to get technical. When are we going for a walk?'

25 June

English writer George Orwell was born on this day in 1903. Among his many famous works is the 1945 novella *Animal Farm,* in which the creatures of Manor Farm attempt to overthrow their human master and create a new society. However, things don't go to plan, and soon the pigs, who had led the revolution, become hungry for power and corrupt. One of them, Napoleon, takes 'nine sturdy puppies' from their mothers, farm dogs Bluebell and Jessie, and promises to educate them. The pups are all but forgotten about – until Napoleon launches an attack on his rival pig Snowball, with the help of 'nine enormous dogs'.

> Silent and terrified, the animals crept back into the barn. In a moment the dogs came bounding back. At first no one had been able to imagine where these creatures came from, but the problem was soon solved: they were the puppies whom Napoleon had taken away from their mothers and reared privately. Though not yet full-grown, they were huge dogs, and as fierce-looking as wolves. It was noticed that they wagged their tails to him in the same way as the other dogs had been used to do to Mr Jones.

26 June

I am secretly afraid of animals – of all animals except dogs, and even of some dogs. I think it is because of the Usness in their eyes, with the underlying not-usness which belies it, and is so tragic a reminder of the lost age when we human beings branched off and left them; left them to eternal inarticulateness and slavery.

Why? Their eyes seem to ask us.

– Edith Wharton, *Quaderno dello Studente*

27 June

Today's dog is Sharik, who features in Mikhail Bulgakov's novella *The Heart of a Dog*, a parable about the Russian Revolution originally written in 1925, but not published until 1968 (and not until 1987 in the former Soviet Union). It tells the story of a stray dog who is taken in by an apparently kindly surgeon, who names him Sharik ('little ball'). At first Sharik is happy, growing healthy and plump, but then he realizes that his new master has a sinister motive. Sharik is sedated and the surgeon operates on him, giving him a human pituitary gland and testicles. As he recovers from the surgery, the dog gradually becomes a human – and chaos ensues.

28 June

Our dog today is the narrator of Walter Emanuel's 1919 novella *A Dog Day*, a playful depiction of a dog's daily activities from dawn to dusk. Each entry is time-stamped ('10 to 10.15: Wagged tail') and all are delightful.

> 7.00: Down to supper. Ate it, but without much relish. I am off my feed to-day.
> 7.15: Ate kittens' supper. But I do wish they would not give them that eternal fish. I am sick of it.
> 7.16: Sick of it in the garden.
> 7.25: Nasty feeling of lassitude comes over me, with loss of all initiative, so I decide to take things quietly, and lie down by the kitchen fire. Sometimes I think that I am not the dog that I was.
> 8.00: Hooray! Appetite returning.
> 8.01: Ravenous.
> 8.02: Have one of the nicest pieces of coal I have ever come across.

29 June

Today's dogs are Brom and Khina (Bromine and Quinine), the beloved pet Dachshunds of Russian playwright and writer Anton Chekhov. His sister Maria named them after the elements found in his medicine bag. Khina was his particular favourite, and Chekhov's biographer Ernest J Simmons notes:

Khina grew so fat that her belly almost dragged on the ground. Chekhov pretended that she suffered from this, and when Khina put her paw on his knee and gazed sadly into his eyes, he would change the expression on his face and in a pitying voice carry on a long monologue with the dog, beginning, 'Khina Markovna! Sufferer that you are! You ought to be in the hospital!' And the guests would roar over this simulated doctor's advice to his canine patient.

30 June

English novelist Winston Graham was born on this day in 1908. Today's dog is Garrick, canine companion of Demelza, who appears in his popular *Poldark* books.

If Demelza grew and developed, Garrick was a beanstalk. When he came he had been more of a puppy than anyone thought, and with proper food he enlarged so rapidly that one began to suspect the sheep dog in his ancestry. The sparse black curls of his coat remained and his lack of tail made him curiously clumsy and unbalanced. He took a great fancy to Jud, who couldn't bear the sight of him, and the ungainly dog followed the bald old rascal everywhere.

JULY

July is here, and any self-respecting dog knows that the best way to spend this golden, sunny month is with one's head sticking out of the car window, ears flapping in the breeze, ideally en route to the beach. And if you're in need of some inspiration for a book to take with you, you'll be spoiled for choice this month. We'll be meeting a dog who thinks he can fly (14 July) and a canine philosopher (3 July), along with two poodles (7 and 23 July), two wolves (19 and 20 July) and a very well-loved toy (16 July).

1 July

Back on 3 February, we met Basket(s), the poodle(s) owned by Gertrude Stein and Alice B Toklas. Today's dog is another from their household, the mischievous Polybe, who lived with them while they were in Mallorca during the First World War. In letters, Stein describes Polybe dancing with the local wild dogs under the moonlight. He also appears in a number of works she created during this time – although, as one might expect, in a rather abstract fashion, as in this piece 'Polybe in Port: A Curtain Raiser'.

Polybe is an ornament.

He is not thinner.

He likes the water now.

This I do not believe.

Neither do I believe there was any intention to go that way. Which way do you mean. Polybe does not remember. Me. Yes. The house. Yes. The servant. Yes. You are not mistaken.

We are not mistaken.

2 July

On the last night of the marriage, my husband and I went to the ballet. We sat behind a blind man; his guide dog, in harness, lay beside him in the aisle of the theatre. I could not keep my attention on the performance; instead, I watched the guide dog watch the performance. Throughout the evening, the dog's head moved, following the dancers across the stage. Every so often the dog would whimper slightly.

'Because he can hear high notes we can't?' my husband said.

'No,' I said, 'because he was disappointed in the choreography.'

– Amy Hempel, *The Dog of the Marriage*

3 July

Czech writer Franz Kafka was born on this day in 1883. He is best known for his mind-boggling surrealist novels, such as *The Trial* and *The Metamorphosis*, but today we will be looking at his 1922 short story 'Investigations of a Dog'. Told in first person by an unnamed pooch, the story is a collection of musings on the sometimes confounding nature of doggishness (or 'dogdom') and its place in the day-to-day world.

I know that it is not one of the virtues of dogdom to share with others food that one has once gained possession of. Life is hard, the earth stubborn, science rich in knowledge but poor in practical results: anyone who has food keeps it to himself; that is not selfishness, but the opposite, dog law, the unanimous decision of the people, the outcome of their victory over egoism, for the possessors are always in a minority.

4 July

American author Nathaniel Hawthorne was born on this day in 1804. To mark his birthday, today's dog is Tiger, who makes a brief appearance in a journal entry written by Hawthorne in 1838.

A rough-looking, sunburnt, soiled-shirted, odd, middle-aged little man came to the house a day or two ago, seeking work. [...] He made a long eulogy on his dog Tiger, yesterday, insisting on his good moral character, his not being quarrelsome, his docility, and all other excellent qualities that a huge, strong, fierce mastiff could have. Tiger is the bully of the village, and keeps all the other dogs in awe. His aspect is very spirited, trotting massively along, with his tail elevated and his head likewise. 'When he sees a dog that's anything near his size,— he's apt to growl a little,' – Tiger had the marks of a battle on him – 'yet he's a good dog.'

5 July

New Zealand children's book writer Lynley Dodd was born on this day in 1941. In her honour, today's dog is her delightful creation Hairy Maclary, a scruffy terrier with a tendency to get into scrapes. He first appeared in 1983 in *Hairy Maclary from Donaldson's Dairy*, and has popped up in numerous books ever since, along with his cast of doggy friends, including a huge mastiff named Hercules Morse and a Dalmatian called Bottomley Potts.

6 July

Today's dog is Lorelei, who appears in Carolyn Pankhurst's 2004 novel *Lorelei's Secret.* The book tells the story of Paul, whose wife Lexy dies in a mysterious accident witnessed only by Lorelei, their pet dog. Desperate to find out what happened, Paul embarks on an investigation, hoping to find a way of communicating with Lorelei and learning from her what really happened that day.

> But in the evenings when I sit with Lorelei and she gazes up at me with her wide, inscrutable eyes, I wonder what she would tell me if she could. Sometimes I get down on the carpet with her to speak to her softly and ask her my questions while I rest my hand upon her great furrowed head. More than once I have awakened to find that I have fallen asleep with my head on the wide, rough expanse of her side.

7 July

Carlo Collodi's children's novel *The Adventures of Pinocchio* was originally published in serial form – and the first part came out on this day in 1881. Today's dog is Medoro, the elegantly attired poodle who acts as the stagecoach driver for the Fairy with Turquoise Hair.

The Fairy, then striking her hands together, made two little claps, and a magnificent Poodle appeared, walking upright on his hind legs exactly as if he had been a man.

He was in the full-dress livery of a coachman. On his head he had a three-cornered cap braided with gold, his curly white wig came down onto his shoulders, he had a chocolate-coloured waistcoat with diamond buttons, and two large pockets to contain the bones that his mistress gave him at dinner. He had besides a pair of short crimson velvet breeches, silk stockings, cut-down shoes, and hanging behind him a species of umbrella case made of blue satin, to put his tail into when the weather was rainy.

8 July

Our dog today is Belle, star of Cécile Aubry's children's book *Belle et Sébastien*, which was also a popular French TV series. Belle is a white Pyrenean mountain dog who has been sold from owner to owner until finally escaping to live in the wilderness of the mountains. Sébastien is a young boy who was born on the mountain and adopted by some local villagers. When rumours start buzzing about a huge dog, a 'beast' that is roaming on the mountain, Sébastien doesn't imagine a threat, but a potential friend – and sets out in search of her.

> Sébastien wiped his eyes with the back of his hand. There she was, standing tall, motionless save for the plume of her tail as it beat the air. Vapour came out of the half-open chops with their long black outline; two more black lines made her eyes stand out in the golden whiteness of her fur. She saw him. She bent her head towards him. Was she going to jump? He no longer felt any fear, and if he too stood still it was because an unknown force compelled him to hold his ground before the animal now watching him. He called to her very softly:
>
> 'Belle ...'

9 July

The wildly successful *Northern Lights* by Philip Pullman was first published on this day in 1995, the first in his hugely popular trilogy *His Dark Materials.* The writer has two dogs, beautiful cockapoos named Coco and Mixie – and dogs do also appear in the pages of his books, most often in the form of daemons – the souls of the human characters. In Pullman's magical world, souls exist outside the body as daemons, and take on animal forms as they accompany their humans through their lives. A child's daemon can change shape at will, according to their mood, but as a person matures, their daemon takes on a fixed shape, said to represent some aspect of their personality.

> [The Steward] smoothed his hair over his ears with both palms and said something to his daemon. He was a servant, so she was a dog, but a superior servant, so a superior dog. In fact, she had the form of a red setter. The daemon seemed suspicious, and cast around as if she'd sensed an intruder, but didn't make for the wardrobe, to Lyra's intense relief.

10 July

French writer Marcel Proust was born on this day in 1871. He bought a dog as a gift for his friend and lover, the composer Reynaldo Hahn, and Hahn in turn named the pup Zadig in honour of Voltaire's novella of the same name. It doesn't get much more literary than that.

11 July

American author E B White was born on this day in 1899. While perhaps best known for writing about spiders (*Charlotte's Web*) and mice (*Stuart Little*), he also loved dogs (as we have already seen on 12 April). The below comes from an essay he wrote in 1957.

> I bought a puppy last week in the outskirts of Boston and drove him to Maine in a rented Ford that looked like a sculpin. There had been talk in our family of getting a 'sensible' dog this time, and my wife and I had gone over the list of sensible dogs, and had even ventured once or twice into the company of sensible dogs. A friend had a litter of Labradors, and there were other opportunities. But after a period of uncertainty and waste motion my wife suddenly exclaimed one evening, 'Oh, let's just get a dachshund!' She had had a glass of wine, and I could see that the truth was coming out. Her tone was one of exasperation laced with affection.

12 July

I live here: 'Wessex' is my name,
I am a dog known rather well:
I guard the house; but how that came
To be my lot I cannot tell.

– Thomas Hardy, 'A Popular Personage at Home'

13 July

> You get a dog on your mind, it seems to fill up the whole space. Everything you do reminds you of that dog.
>
> – Phyllis Reynolds Naylor, *Shiloh*

14 July

Scottish writer Jane Welsh Carlyle was born on this day in 1801. The wife of author Thomas Carlyle, she is known as a great letter-writer, exchanging epistles that spark with wit and warmth. She had a dog named Nero, whose escapades often featured in her letters. In March 1850, she described a particularly alarming incident.

> He has had another wonderful escape that dog! I begin to think he 'bears a charmed life'. This time the danger was entirely of his own seeking. Imagine his taking it into his head that he could *fly* – like the birds – if he tried! and actually trying it – out at the Library window! For a first attempt his success was not so bad; for he fairly cleared the area spikes – and tho' he *did* plash down on the pavement at the feet of an astonished Boy he broke no bones, was only quite stunned. He gave us a horrid fright however. [...] I sat down on the floor and laid my insensible dog over my knees, but could see no *breakage* – only a stun. So I took him to bed with me – *under* the clothes – and in an hour's time he was as brisk and active as ever. I wonder if he intends to persevere in learning to fly – for I don't think either my own or my maid's nerves can stand it!

15 July

Scottish naturalist and writer Gavin Maxwell was born on this day in 1914. Though his bestselling memoir *Ring of Bright Water* is largely concerned with otters, in its earlier chapters he describes the deep bond he shared with his dog, a black-and-white spaniel named Jonnie, who joined him on shark-fishing expeditions.

> Many people find an especial attachment for a dog whose companionship has bridged widely different phases in their lives, and so it was with Jonnie; he and his forebears had spanned my boyhood, maturity and the way years, and though since then I had found little leisure nor much inclination for shooting, Jonnie adapted himself placidly to a new role, and I remember how during the shark fishery years he would, unprotesting, arrange himself to form a pillow for my head in the well of an open boat as it tossed and pitched in the waves.

16 July

English writer and illustrator Shirley Hughes was born on this day in 1927. Today's dog is the star of her book *Dogger*, a toy dog owned by a little boy named Dave. Well-loved, with his fur slightly worn, Dogger is Dave's constant companion – until the unthinkable happens and he goes missing. Beautifully illustrated and undeniably charming, *Dogger* has captured the hearts of millions.

17 July

Today's dog is Maude, the faithful and comforting pooch who appears in Claire Fuller's 2021 novel *Unsettled Ground.*

> They watch Maude outside, digging in what once might have been flower beds, now overgrown with weeds. Bridget puts her cigarette in her mouth and raps hard on the window. 'Oy!' she calls, and Maude stops to look at them and then goes back to her digging. 'Best keep her outside,' Bridget says.

18 July

Jane Austen died on this day in 1817. Today's dog merits just the briefest of mentions in her novel *Persuasion,* but the pooch unwittingly creates one in a series of excruciating situations for Anne, the novel's long-suffering heroine. Anne and her younger sister Mary are invited for a walk by Mary's sisters-in-law, the Miss Musgroves, while Mary's husband Charles is out shooting with Captain Wentworth – who just so happens to be Anne's former fiancé. Anne agrees to go along on the walk, assuming it will just be the four women – and then the dog interferes with her plan.

> Just as they were setting off, the gentlemen returned. They had taken out a young dog, which had spoilt their sport, and sent them back early. Their time, and strength, and spirits were, therefore, exactly ready for this walk, and they entered into it with pleasure. Could Anne

have foreseen such a junction, she would have staid at home; but, from some feelings of interest and curiosity, she fancied now that it was too late to retract, and the whole six set forward together in the direction chosen by the Miss Musgroves.

19 July

Today's canine comes from Aesop's fable 'The Shepherd Boy and the Wolf', also known as 'The Boy Who Cried Wolf'. It tells the story of a young shepherd boy who, bored one day while tending his sheep, decides to play a trick on the local villagers by pretending he has seen a wolf. He shouts out 'Wolf! Wolf!', and the villagers come running to his aid, much to his amusement. He repeats the hoax more than once, which understandably starts to irritate people. When the day comes when a wolf really does approach his herd, nobody responds to the boy's cry for help, assuming he is lying again. The wolf devours all the sheep; in some tellings, he also gobbles up the boy for good measure.

20 July

American author Cormac McCarthy was born on this day in 1933. In his honour, our canine today is another wolf, this time the nameless she-wolf from his 1994 novel *The Crossing*. The novel's protagonist, Billy, learns that the wolf has been preying on cattle near his family's homestead, and sets out to track her.

You want to catch this wolf, the old man said. Maybe you want the skin so you can get some money. Maybe you can buy some boots or something like that. You can do that. But where is the wolf? The wolf is like the copo de nieve.

Snowflake.

Snowflake. You catch the snowflake but when you look in your hand you don't have it no more. Maybe you see this dechado. But before you can see it it is gone. If you want to see it you have to see it on its own ground. If you catch it you lose it.

21 July

Welsh novelist Sarah Waters was born on this day in 1966. Today's dog is Gyp from her 2009 novel *The Little Stranger*.

There came again the gruff excited barking of a dog – alarmingly close, this time – and a second later an elderly black Labrador burst from somewhere into the passage and began hurtling towards me. I stood still with my bag raised while it barked and pranced around me, and soon a young woman appeared behind it, saying mildly. 'All right, you idiotic creature, that's enough! Gyp! Enough!'

22 July

As it is now the height of summer, our dogs today are Theseus's hounds in *A Midsummer Night's Dream*. Here, he boasts about how tuneful their barking is.

My hounds are bred out of the Spartan kind
So flewed, so sanded, and their heads are hung
With ears that sweep away the morning dew,
Crook-kneed and dew-lapped, like Thessalian bulls;
Slow in pursuit, but matched in mouth like bells,
Each under each. A cry more tuneable
Was never holla'd to, nor cheered with horn.

– Act IV, Scene I

23 July

Trudie was an exceptionally silly-looking dog, a large, black French poodle who moved exactly as if she had been animated by Walt Disney: a kind of lollop that was emphasised by her large floppy ears at the front end and a short stubby tail with a bit of topiary work on the end.

– Douglas Adams, *The Salmon of Doubt*

24 July

French writer Alexandre Dumas was born on this day in 1802. In *Mary Stuart*, his historical account of the life of Mary, Queen of Scots, he describes the unshakeable faithfulness of her little Maltese terrier, who refused to leave his mistress even as she was executed. It is a devastating image.

> At few moments later, as the executioner was untying the Queen's garters he spied the poor little creature cowering beneath her petticoat and pulled him from his hiding-place, but the terrified animal escaped from his grasp and took refuge between his dead mistress' shoulders and her head, which had been deposited beside her body, where he crouched whining pitifully.

25 July

Today's dog is the sweet and loyal Pepper, who appears in William Hope Hodgson's cult horror novel *The House on the Borderland*, which was published in 1908. Two men on holiday discover a strange chasm in the ground while on a fishing trip in a remote area. Within it, they find an old journal, which opens as follows:

> I am an old man. I live here in this ancient house surrounded by huge, unkempt gardens.
>
> The peasantry, who inhabit the wilderness beyond, say that I am mad. That is because I will have nothing to do with them. I live here alone with my old sister, who is also my housekeeper. We keep no servants – I hate them. I have one friend, a dog; yes, I would sooner have old Pepper than the rest of Creation together. He, at least, understands me – and has sense enough to leave me alone when I am in my dark moods.

26 July

On this day in 1926, Vita Sackville-West gave Virginia Woolf a cocker spaniel puppy, whom she named Pinka (sometimes written Pinker). Woolf often wrote about Pinka in her letters and diaries, and the dog was fond of curling up in Leonard Woolf's chair while he was away, keeping her mistress company as she wrote and read.

27 July

She was trusted and valued by her father, loved and courted by all dogs, cats, children, and poor people, and slighted and neglected by everybody else.

– Anne Brontë, *The Tenant of Wildfell Hall*

28 July

English writer and illustrator Beatrix Potter was born on this day in 1866. She's known for her many delightful animal creations, including those we met on 4 March and 24 May. Today, our dog is Duchess, who appears in *The Tale of the Pie and the Patty-Pan.* A cat named Ribby invites Duchess to come for tea, promising to serve a delicious pie. Although Duchess accepts, she becomes concerned that Ribby might serve her mouse pie, which she doesn't want to eat. Rather than explaining, Duchess concocts an elaborate plan to replace Ribby's pie with one she has baked herself, but things don't quite go to plan …

29 July

We met Toto back on 17 May, and he will, of course, always be the most important dog in Oz. But today's canine is King Dox of Foxville, who appears in Frank L Baum's 1909 novel *The Road to Oz,* the fifth in his *Oz* series. King Dox has the ability to transform the head of anyone he meets into that of a fox – but he can't turn them back.

> As he spoke the King waved his paw towards the boy, and at once the pretty curls and fresh round face and big blue eyes were gone, while in their place a fox's head appeared upon Button-Bright's shoulders – a hairy head with a sharp nose, pointed ears and keen little eyes.

30 July

Emily Brontë was born on this day in 1818. The Brontë family kept several dogs, but Emily had a particularly strong bond with one named Keeper. Brontë biographer Clement King Shorter wrote:

> The tawny, strong-limbed 'Keeper' [was] Emily's favourite: he was so completely under her control, she could quite easily make him spring and roar like a lion. She taught him this kind of occasional play without any coercion.

31 July

American writer William Maxwell died on this day in 2000. Today's dog is Trixie from his novel *So Long, See You Tomorrow,* a faithful and gentle hound who waits patiently at the mailbox each day for her young master to get home, neither of them knowing that they will soon be separated.

> When it is almost time for Cletus to come home from school the dog squeezes herself under the gates and trots off up the road to the mailboxes, where she settles down in a place that she has made for herself in the high grass with her chin resting on her fourpaws.

And when he arrives:

> With the dog loping along beside him he pedals for dear life over the final stretch of road. The dog waits each time until he has closed the gate and then she trots on ahead importantly, as if by himself the boy wouldn't know the way home. […] The dog follows Cletus up onto the porch, leaving her neat footprints wherever she has been.

AUGUST

With the long, hot days of August, a certain lethargy can overtake us, so this month we have an abundance of high-energy puppies to liven things up, from a giant pup (8 August) to one so tiny it could be mistaken for a scrap of cloth (25 August). If you need an escape from a summer heat, take a chilling trip to Manderley (5 August) or cool off in the icy landscapes of Moominland (9 August).

We also have some brave and loyal watchdogs (15 and 24 August), along with a dog who *is* a watch (12 August), just to keep things interesting.

1 August

American author Herman Melville was born on this day in 1819. Although his most famous creation is the whale at the heart of his 1851 epic *Moby-Dick,* he had some wise words to say about dogs (and horses) in his 1849 novel *Redburn.*

> No philosophers so thoroughly comprehend us as dogs and horses. They see through us at a glance.

2 August

Chilean-American author Isabel Allende was born on this day in 1942. Our dog today is the gentle Barrabás from her family saga *The House of the Spirits,* published in 1982. The novel opens with the arrival of Barrabás as a puppy, delivered to the Trueba family in miserable condition after the death of Clara's Uncle Marcos.

> After he had had a bath, he was found to be black, with a square head, long legs and short hair. Nana suggested cutting off his tail to make him more refined, but Clara had a tantrum that degenerated into an asthma attack and no one ever mentioned it again. Barrabás kept his tail, which in time grew to be as long as a golf club and developed a life all its own that led to lamps and china being swept from tabletops. [...] The dog had a seemingly unlimited capacity for growth. Within six months he was the size of a sheep, and at the end of a year he was as big as a colt. In desperation the family began to question whether he would ever stop growing and whether he really was a dog.

3 August

Our dog today is Nerak from Florence Engel Randall's 1976 mystery novel *A Watcher in the Woods*. The story's narrator, Jan, is 15 years old when her family moves to a new town. Their home is a large house on the outskirts, surrounded by woodland. From the moment they arrive, Jan has a sense of something watching them from within the trees. She learns that a young girl named Karen who used to live in their house vanished without a trace fifty years before. When Jan's little sister Ellie is gifted a puppy, they find themselves compelled to name it Nerak, though they aren't sure why …

> The picture was Ellie's version of a dog, the head a small circle topped by pointed ears, the body a large circle with four legs and a tail sticking out of it. Underneath, so there would be no mistake, she had printed N E R A K, but evidently without her usual, painstaking care, for each letter except the A was reversed.
>
> 'Mirror writing,' my father exclaimed, surprised. 'You've never done that before, Ellie. Why should you start now?'
>
> Mirror writing, I told myself, appalled. […] Lettering held to a mirror read not from left to right, but from right to left, and Nerak spelled backwards—
>
> I froze.

4 August

Today's pooch is Laddie from Terry Pratchett's 1990 novel *Moving Pictures,* which explores the creation of films in Discworld. It is set in 'Holy Wood' and sees Gaspode, the super-intelligent canine whom we met back on 28 April, encountering the not-so-bright Laddie, a beautiful dog who seems set for stardom, despite not having a tenth of Gaspode's wits.

> Laddie did tricks. Laddie could drink out of bottles, Laddie could bark the number of fingers people held up; so could Gaspode, of course, but it had never occurred to him that such an activity could be rewarded. [...] Laddie could home in on young women who were being taken out for the evening by a hopeful swain and lay his head in their lap and give them such a soulful look that the swain would buy him a saucer of beer and a bag of goldfish-shaped biscuits just in order to impress the prospective loved one. Gaspode had never been able to do that, because he was too short for laps and, anyway, got nothing but disgusting screams if he tried it.

5 August

Rebecca, the iconic Gothic novel by Daphne du Maurier, was first published on this day in 1938. Our dog today is Jasper, one of the spaniels owned by Maxim de Winter. Jasper's sweet nature brings some much-needed warmth as our unnamed heroine explores the chilling world of Manderley.

Two cocker spaniels came from the fireside to greet us. They pawed at Maxim, their long, silken ears strained back with affection, their noses questing his hands, and then they left him and came to me, sniffing at my heels, rather uncertain, rather suspicious. One was the mother, blind in one eye, and soon she had enough of me, and took herself with a grunt to the fire again, but Jasper, the younger, put his nose into my hand, and laid a chin upon my knee, his eyes deep with meaning, his tail a-thump when I stroked his silken ears.

6 August

Dogs are the magicians of the universe. By their presence alone, they transform grumpy people into grinning people, sad people into less sad people; they engender relationship.

– Clarissa Pinkola Estés, *Women Who Run With the Wolves*

7 August

Richard Matheson's post-apocalyptic vampire novel *I Am Legend* was published on this day in 1954. The novel's protagonist, Robert Neville, appears to be the sole survivor of a pandemic that has wiped out the population and turned infected people into vampires. Our dog today is the stray pooch that Neville spots in the street one day. He leaves out food for the poor creature, and their brief encounters provide him with some short-lived relief and joy as he struggles to survive.

The dog came at four. Nevill had almost fallen into a doze as he sat there before the peephole. Then his eyes blinked and focused as the dog came hobbling slowly across the street [...].

He forced himself to sit still and watch. It was incredible, the feeling of warmth and normality it gave him to see the dog slurping up the milk and eating the hamburger, its jaws snapping and popping with relish. He sat there with a gentle smile on his face, a smile he wasn't conscious of. It was such a nice dog.

8 August

Today's dog is the 'dear little puppy' encountered by Alice in Lewis Carroll's 1865 classic *Alice's Adventures in Wonderland.* After eating and drinking various substances that cause her to shrink or grow to different sizes, a miniature Alice encounters an ordinary-sized puppy in the woods – although to her, of course, the creature is huge.

An enormous puppy was looking down at her with large round eyes and feebly stretching out one paw, trying to touch her. 'Poor little thing!' said Alice, in a coaxing tone, and she tried hard to whistle to it; but she was terrible frightened all the time at the thought that it might be hungry, in which case it would be very likely to eat her up in spite of all her coaxing.

9 August

Finnish-Swedish writer, painter and illustrator Tove Jansson was born on this day in 1914. She was a multi-talented artist who is best known for creating the iconic *Moomin* series, and so our dog today is Sorry-oo, a 'thin little dog with a tattered woollen cap pulled deep over his ears', who makes his first appearance in *Moominland Midwinter*.

The moonlight was blue. Sorry-oo sat alone in the snow, howling. He put his muzzle straight up in the air and howled a long and melancholy song.

'Why don't you go to bed?' asked Moomintroll.

Sorry-oo looked at him with eyes that shone green in the moonlight. One ear was pointing straight up while the other listened to one side. His whole face was listening.

Very faintly they could hear the howl of hunting wolves. Sorry-oo nodded bleakly and pulled his woollen cap on again.

'My great, strong brethren,' he whispered. 'How I long to be with them.'

10 August

[The] Thénardiers began to look upon the little girl as a child which they sheltered for charity, and treated her as such. Her clothes being gone, they dressed her in the cast-off garments of the little Thénardiers, that is, in rags. They fed her on the odds and ends, a little better than the dog, and a little worse than the cat. The dog and the cat were her messmates, Cosette ate with them under the table in a wooden dish like theirs.

– Victor Hugo, *Les Misérables*

11 August

English children's writer Enid Blyton was born on this day in 1897. We'll be meeting her most famous canine creation on 11 September, but today our dog is Buster, who appears alongside her lesser-known quintet the Five Find-Outers, whose series opens with *The Mystery of the Burnt Cottage*. Buster is a black Scottish terrier with a fondness for biscuits and potted meat.

'Look – there's that dog again,' said Bets, pointing to the little black Scottie appearing in the garden. He stood sturdily on his squat legs, his ears cocked, looking up at them as if to say, 'Mind me being here?'

'Hallo, Buster!' said Larry, bending down and patting his knee to make the dog come to him. 'You're a nice dog, you are. I wish you were mine. Daisy and I have never had a dog.'

'Nor have I,' said Pip. 'Here, Buster! Bone, Buster? Biscuit, Buster?'

'Woof,' said Buster, in a surprisingly deep voice for such a small dog.

12 August

Norton Juster's children's fantasy novel *The Phantom Tollbooth* was first published on this day in 1961. Our dog today is Tock, a watchdog who joins the novel's hero Milo as he embarks on a journey through the Kingdom of Wisdom, which he reached via a magical tollbooth.

> Milo's eyes opened wide, for there in front of him was a large dog with a perfectly normal head, four feet, and a tail – and the body of a loudly ticking alarm clock.
>
> 'What are you doing here?' growled the watchdog.
>
> 'Just killing time,' replied Milo apologetically. 'You see—'
>
> 'KILLING TIME!' roared the dog – so furiously that his alarm went off. It's bad enough wasting time without killing it.' And he shuddered at the thought.

13 August

English science-fiction writer H G Wells died on this day in 1946. Today's dog comes from his 1897 novel *The Invisible Man*. In the extract below, Griffin – the invisible man himself – describes to another character the moment when he realized that his invisibility might not conceal him from dogs as successfully as it does humans.

At the northward corner of the square a little white dog ran out of the Pharmaceutical Society's offices, and incontinently made for me, nose down.

I had never realised it before, but the nose is to the mind of a dog what the eye is to the mind of a seeing man. Dogs perceive the scent of a man moving as men perceive his visible appearance. This brute began barking and leaping, showing, as it seemed to me only too plainly, that he was aware of me.

14 August

American writer Fred Gipson died on this day in 1973. In his honour, today's dog is the eponymous star of his heartbreaking 1956 children's novel *Old Yeller*, who earns his place in the hearts of the Coates family, working alongside them on their Texas ranch and saving them from all sorts of scrapes, including a bear attack.

We called him Old Yeller. The name had a sort of double meaning. One part meant that his short hair was a dingy yellow, a colour that we called 'yeller' in those days. The other meant that when he opened his head, the sound he let out came closer to being a yell than a bark.

15 August

Today's dogs are Grip, Fang and Wolf, three huge, fearsome guard dogs owned by Farmer Maggot, the shrewd hobbit in J R R Tolkien's *The Fellowship of the Ring.*

[A]s they drew nearer a terrific baying and barking broke out, and a loud voice was heard shouting: 'Grip! Fang! Wolf! Come on, lads!'

Frodo and Sam stopped dead, but Pippin walked on a few paces. The gate opened and three huge dogs came pelting out into the lane, and dashed towards the travellers, barking fiercely. They took no notice of Pippin; but Sam shrank against the wall, while two wolvish-looking dogs sniffed at him suspiciously, and snarled if he moved. The largest and most ferocious of the three halted in front of Frodo, bristling and growling.

16 August

English writer Georgette Heyer was born on this day in 1902. Today's dog, then, is Lufra, who appears in her 1965 Regency romance *Frederica.*

A large and shaggy dog, of indeterminate parentage, was at [Jessamy's] heels; and just as he was apologising to Frederica for having come in when she was entertaining a visitor, this animal advanced with the utmost affability to greet the Marquis. His disposition was friendly, as he showed by the waving of his plumed tail; and his evident intention was to jump up at the guest. But Alverstoke, wise in the ways of dogs, preserved his face from being generously licked, and his exquisitely fashioned coat of Bath Superfine from being smirched by muddy paws, by catching the animals forearms, and holding him at bay. 'Yes, good dog!' he said. 'I'm much obliged to you, but I don't care to have my face licked!'

17 August

English poet Ted Hughes was born on this day in 1930. In his honour, today's dog is Roger, from his 1984 amusing poem 'Roger the Dog'.

Asleep he wheezes at his ease.
He only wakes to scratch his fleas.

18 August

Our dog today is Bella, who appears in Elsa Morante's 1974 Italian bestseller *History*.

[She] danced on greeting you; and, to kiss, she licked you with her rasping tongue; and she laughed with her face and her tail [...]. Bella at times had a special sweetness and melancholy in her hazel eyes, perhaps because she was female.

Her breed, known as Maremma or Abruzzi shepherds, came from Asia, where Bella's ancestors, from the dawn of history, had followed the flocks of the earth's first shepherds. [...] She had a rural mien, full of majesty; her coat was all white, thick, a bit ruffled at times; and she had a kind, jolly face, with a black nose.

19 August

Today's dog is Hermes, who appears in Jostein Gaarder's novel *Sophie's World*. Hermes is the canine companion of philosopher Alberto Knox, and acts as his messenger, delivering letters and postcards to the 15-year-old Sophie as Knox teaches her the history of philosophy.

The next moment a big Labrador pushed its way into the den.

In its mouth it held a big brown envelope which is dropped at Sophie's feet. It all happened so quickly that Sophie had no time to react. A second later she was sitting with the big envelope in her hands – and the golden Labrador had scampered off into the woods again.

[...] So that was his famous messenger! Sophie breathed a sigh of relief. Of course that was why the white envelopes were wet around the edges and had holes in them. Why hadn't she thought of it? Now it made sense to put a cookie or a lump of sugar in the envelope when she wrote to the philosopher.

20 August

Our pooch today is Buller, who appears in Graham Greene's 1978 spy novel *The Human Factor*. Buller is a boxer and delights in any and all company, greeting everyone he encounters with great enthusiasm.

> The door creaked and Castle turned quickly; the square black muzzle of Buller pushed the door fully open, and then he launched his body like a sack of potatoes at Castle's fly. Castle fended him off. 'Down, Buller, down.' A long ribbon of spittle descended Castle's trouser leg. [...] Buller began to bark spasmodically and wriggle his haunches, like a dog with worms, moving backward toward the door.
>
> 'Be quiet, Buller.'
>
> 'He only wants a walk.'
>
> [...] 'Stop it, Buller. Stop.' Buller was licking his private parts with the gusto of an alderman drinking soup.

21 August

Our dog today is the Akita Abraham, from Matt Haig's 2017 novel *How to Stop Time*. He is adopted by the novels' protagonist Tom Hazard – a history teacher in a London secondary school who just happens to have been alive since the 1500s.

> Every other dog in the place is barking. But this one is just lying in its undersized basket. It is a strange grey creature with sapphire eyes. The dog, I feel, is too dignified for such modern garishness, a wolf out of its time. I relate.

22 August

American poet and writer Dorothy Parker was born on this day in 1893. Her delightful poem 'Verse for a Certain Dog' switches playfully between extolling said dog's virtues and trying to control its typically doggish behaviour.

> Such glorious faith as fills your limpid eyes,
> Dear little friend of mine, I never knew.
> All-innocent you are, and yet all-wise.
> (For heaven's sake, stop worrying that shoe!)
> You look about, and all you see is fair;
> This mighty globe was made for you alone.
> Of all the thunderous ages, you're the heir.
> (Get off the pillow with that dirty bone!)

A skeptic world you face with steady gaze;
High in young pride you hold your noble head;
Gayly you meet the rush of roaring days.
(Must you eat puppy biscuit on the bed?)
Lancelike your courage, gleaming swift and strong,
Yours the white rapture of a wingèd soul,
Yours is a spirit like a May-day song.
(God help you, if you break the goldfish bowl!)

'Whatever is, is good,' your gracious creed.
You wear your joy of living like a crown.
Love lights your simplest act, your every deed.
(Drop it, I tell you—put that kitten down!)
You are God's kindliest gift of all,—a friend.
Your shining loyalty unflecked by doubt,
You ask but leave to follow to the end.
(Couldn't you wait until I took you out?)

23 August

It was said that a new person had appeared on the sea-front: a lady with a little dog. Dmitri Dmitrich Gurov, who had by then been a fortnight at Yalta, and so was fairly at home there, had begun to take an interest in new arrivals. Sitting in Verney's pavilion, he saw, walking on the sea-front, a fair-haired young lady of medium height, wearing a beret; a white Pomeranian dog was running behind her.

And afterwards he met her in the public gardens and in the square several times a day. She was walking alone, always wearing the same beret, and always with the same white dog; no one knew who she was, and every one called her simply 'the lady with the dog'.

– Anton Chekhov, 'The Lady with the Dog'

24 August

Although the precise date of the 79 CE eruption of Mount Vesuvius and consequent devastation of Pompeii has never been successfully established, for many centuries historians believed that the event took place on 24 August. While this date has now been thrown into question, our dog today is Pompeiian nonetheless. The House of the Tragic Poet is one of Pompeii's most famous buildings, and its remains contain detailed mosaics – including one in the vestibule depicting a dog, poised and ready to pounce, the tiles emblazoned with the words 'CAVE CANEM' ('Beware of the dog').

25 August

[T]here was a snuffling noise in the passage and through the door came an object which in the dim light he was at first not able to identify. It looked something like a pen-wiper and something like a piece of hearthrug. A second and keener inspection revealed it as a Pekingese puppy.

– P G Wodehouse, *Tales from the Drones Club*

26 August

Today is International Dog Day, so it seems fitting that our dog of the day is particularly magnificent: Cavall (also spelled Cafall), the favourite hunting dog of the legendary King Arthur. Cavall took part in the famous hunt for the wild boar Twrch Trwyth. During the hunt, he was said to have left his pawprint on a stone. Arthur built a cairn of stones beneath this one, and it is said that if anyone ever removed the stone bearing Cavall's pawprint from the mound, it would be found back in its rightful place the next day.

27 August

In her highly praised 1994 book *Bird by Bird: Some Instructions on Writing and Life,* American author Anne Lamott gives the following wise advice for would-be writers struggling to focus their practice:

> Try looking at your mind as a wayward puppy that you are trying to paper train. You don't drop-kick a puppy into the neighbour's yard every time it piddles on the floor. You just keep bringing it back to the newspaper. So I keep trying gently to bring my mind back to what is really there to be seen, maybe to be seen and noted with a kind of reverence.

28 August

> A puppy is but a dog, plus high spirits, minus common sense.
>
> – Agnes Repplier, *In the Dozy Hours*

29 August

Our dog today is the gentle Anax from Iris Murdoch's 1993 novel *The Green Knight.*

> The dog, whose name was Anax, a distinguished and unusual collie with blue eyes, and long silver-grey fur blotched with black and white, came bounding back to the two women.

30 August

Frankenstein author Mary Shelley was born on this day in 1797. Today's canines are the team of dogs who are glimpsed in the novel's early pages, pulling a sledge driven by an unnervingly large figure …

> About two o'clock the mist cleared away, and we beheld, stretched out in every direction, vast and irregular plains of ice, which seemed to have no end. Some of my comrades groaned, and my own mind began to grow watchful with anxious thoughts, when a strange sight suddenly attracted our attention, and diverted

our solicitude from our own situation. We perceived a low carriage, fixed on a sledge and drawn by dogs, pass on towards the north, at the distance of half a mile: a being which had the shape of a man, but apparently of gigantic stature, sat in the sledge, and guided the dogs. We watched the rapid progress of the traveller with our telescopes, until he was lost among the distant inequalities of the ice.

31 August

Then what happened, a couple of days later I saw Jane laying on her stomach next to the swimming pool, at the club, and I said hello to her. I knew she lived in the house next to ours, but I'd never conversed with her before or anything. She gave me the big freeze when I said hello that day, though. I had a helluva time convincing her that I didn't give a good goddam *where* her dog relieved himself. He could do it in the living room, for all I cared.

– J D Salinger, *The Catcher in the Rye*

SEPTEMBER

As summer draws to a close and children return to school, we mark the change in the calendar with not one but two Spots starring in children's books (3 and 7 September), as well as paying tribute to one of the most famous literary dogs of all, Timothy from *The Famous Five*. We'll also start edging into spooky season with some pooches from the scarier side of life, including the truly terrifying Cujo (8 September).

And, to keep things interesting, we'll be meeting a dog owned by a star (13 September), as well as a hound who turns into one (6 September).

1 September

Today's dog is Your Dog (or My Dog, depending on who is speaking), the loyal pal of Angelina Sicco, protagonist of monster novel *Feast While You Can* by Mikaella Clements and Onjuli Datta. As Angelina has to battle with a strange creature that seems to have crept from a pit outside her hometown, Cadenze, and taken up residence in, well, *her*, her faithful pooch does her best to help.

> Angelina had found My Dog tied up and abandoned by the side of the highway, a young hip-high mutt with a feathery tail and her head bowed to the ground. [...] After a few good meals, My Dog revealed herself to be a loving, slobbering fool. She followed Angelina with devotion, happiest when running at her heels with no clue where she was headed. [...] At first Angelina and Patrick had both called her The Dog, and then as allegiances formed, she became Your Dog (Patrick's preferred usage) or My Dog (Angelina's). People in town caught on and paused in the street to say, *Hello, Your Dog!* and *Isn't Your Dog a good girl?*

2 September

Gloves and shoes; she had a passion for gloves; but her own daughter, her Elizabeth, cared not a straw for either of them.

Not a straw, she thought, going on up Bond Street to a shop where they kept flowers for her when she gave a party. Elizabeth really cared for her dog most of all.

– Virginia Woolf, *Mrs Dalloway*

3 September

Today's dog may well be the first literary dog encountered by many readers of a certain age: Spot, the lovely black-and-white pooch who appears in the *Dick and Jane* books. First published in the 1930s – the *Dick and Jane* series were developed to help children learn to read, with simple stories and repetitive language.

4 September

Our dog today is Mr Bones from Paul Auster's 1999 novella *Timbuktu*. Mr Bones's master, Willy G Christmas, is dying, and the anxious dog is worried about what that might mean.

> What was a poor dog to do? Mr Bones had been with Willy since his earliest days as a pup, and by now it was next to impossible for him to imagine a world that did not have his master in it. Every thought, every memory, every particle of the earth and air was saturated with Willy's presence. Habits die hard, and no doubt there's some truth to the adage about old dogs and new tricks, but it was more than just love or devotion that caused Mr Bones to dread what was coming. It was pure ontological terror. Subtract Willy from the world, and the odds were that the world itself would cease to exist.

5 September

In her 1988 novel *Carmen Dog*, Carol Emshwiller imagines a world where animals begin turning into women – and women start transforming into animals. Today's dog, Pooch, finds herself transforming into a young woman – while her mistress appears to be turning into a snapping turtle.

> Pooch is doing the best she can for her foster family. (The mistress has taken to drink and sleeps a good bit of the day, but bites out viciously if provoked. Not that she hasn't done something of the sort to some degree

all her life, but before it had usually been a quick slap.) Pooch now does the shopping as well as the laundry, diapering, and much of the cooking, though she is hardly as old as the oldest child she's looking after. Pooch, who had always been smiling and playful, now has become serious and sad, watching over everything with her big, golden-brown, colour-blind eyes.

6 September

Today's dog is Laelaps, a hunting hound found in Greek mythology. Owned by the Athenian princess Procris, Laelaps was said to never fail to catch whatever he was hunting. Procris's husband decided to use Laelaps to hunt the Teumessian fox, which was supposedly impossible to catch. As Laelaps couldn't fail, but the fox couldn't be caught, the chase went on and on – until Zeus turned them both into stone and threw them into the night sky to become the constellations Canis Major and Canis Minor.

7 September

Our dog today is another Spot from the world of children's books, but this one is the star of the show rather than a supporting character. English writer and illustrator Eric Hill was born on this day in 1927, and one of his most famous creations is surely the always loveable Spot the dog. This happy little yellow puppy with his iconic brown spot is instantly recognisable the world over, and has even starred in his own TV series.

8 September

From the adorable to the downright terrifying. *Cujo* by Stephen King was first published on this day in 1981. It tells the story of a rabid Saint Bernard who goes on a chaotic killing spree across his hometown.

> And a moment later Cujo's foam-covered, twisted face popped up outside her window, only inches away, like a horror-movie monster that has decided to give the audience the ultimate thrill by coming right out of the screen. She could see his huge, heavy teeth. And again there was that swooning, terrible feeling that the dog was looking at *her*, not at a woman who just happened to be trapped in her car with her little boy, but at *Donna Trenton*, as if he had just been hanging around, waiting for her to show up.

9 September

Russian writer Leo Tolstoy was born on this day in 1828. Today's dog is Laska, from his 1878 tragic masterpiece *Anna Karenina.*

> Old Laska, who had not yet quite digested her joy at her master's return and had run out to bark in the yard, now came back, bringing a smell of fresh air with her into the room and, wagging her tail, she approached him and putting her head under his hand whined plaintively, asking to be patted.

10 September

American poet and essayist Mary Oliver was born on this day in 1935. Celebrated for her nature writing and remarkable use of imagery, Oliver can write about animals like nobody else.

> And we are caught by the old affinity, a joyfulness – his great and seemly pleasure in the physical world. Because of the dog's joyfulness, our own is increased. It is no small gift. It is not the least reason why we should honour as well as love the dog of our own life, and the dog down the street, and all the dogs not yet born. What would the world be like without music or rivers or the green and tender grass? What would this world be like without dogs?

11 September

Enid Blyton's first *Famous Five* novel, *Five on a Treasure Island* was published on this day in 1942. Today's dog is, of course, Timmy (or Timothy), the fifth member of the five, who joins Julian, Dick, Anne and George on all their adventures.

> 'This is Timothy,' [George] said. 'Don't you think he is simply perfect?'
>
> As a dog, Timothy was far from perfect. He was the wrong shape, his head was too big, his ears were too pricked, his tail was too long and it was quite impossible to say what kind of a dog he was supposed to be. But he was such a mad, friendly, clumsy, laughable creature that every one of the children adored him at once.

12 September

Today's dog is one of a quartet of four animals who team up in the fairy tale 'The Bremen Town Musicians' by the Brothers Grimm. Realizing that they are growing old and about to be turned out (or worse) by their masters, a dog, a donkey, a cat and a cockerel decide to join forces and start a new career as musicians. Before they reach the town of Bremen, where they hope to make their fortunes, however, they come across a house where some robbers are living, and concoct a plan to get rid of the robbers and enjoy the place for themselves.

> The ass was to place his forefeet on the window-sill, the dog was to get on the ass's back, the cat on the top of the dog, and lastly the cock was to fly up and perch on the cat's head. When that was done, at a given signal they all began to perform their music. The ass brayed, the dog barked, the cat mewed and the cock crowed; then they burst through into the room, breaking all the panes of glass. The robbers fled at the dreadful sound; they thought it was some goblin, and fled to the wood in the utmost terror.

13 September

Our dog today is Maf (short for Mafia Honey), hero of Andrew O'Hagan's 2010 novel *The Life and Opinions of Maf the Dog, and of His Friend Marilyn Monroe*. As the title suggests, the novel is a fictionalized account of the life of Marilyn Monroe's pet dog Maf, who was gifted to her by none other than Frank Sinatra.

> Frank's great joke was to place me inside the apartment and let me find my way to Marilyn. The door was open. I stepped over a pair of stiletto shoes covered in bright grey rhinestones – *Ferragamo*, it said inside them – and stopped to nibble the strap of a Pucci handbag that leaned against a drinks trolley. [...] She lifted me into her arms and kissed me as if I was the returning hero, and I did feel special, you know, for a moment, held up high by Marilyn like the dog who finally worked things out and made it home.

14 September

Today's dog is Norma, who makes a brief but memorable appearance fighting off a hideous mysterious reptile in a strange dream recounted by Ippolít Teréntyev in Fyodor Dostoevsky's novel *The Idiot*.

> Then, my mother opened the door and called Norma, our dog – a huge, shaggy, black Newfoundland; it died five years ago. It rushed into the room and stopped

short before the reptile. The creature stopped too, but still wriggled and scraped the ground with its paws and tail. Animals cannot feel the terror of the mysterious, unless I'm mistaken, but at that moment it seemed to me that there was something very extraordinary in Norma's terror, as though there were something uncanny in it, as though the dog too felt that there was something ominous, some mystery in it.

15 September

Celebrated English crime writer Agatha Christie was born on this day in 1890. Today's dog is Bob, who appears in Christie's Poirot novel *Dumb Witness*, published in 1937.

The terrier had continued to bark in some sequestered spot. Now the sound suddenly increased in volume. With a crescendo of barking he could be heard galloping across the hall.

'*Who's* come into the house? *I'll* tear him limb from limb,' was clearly the 'burden of his song'.

He arrived in the doorway, sniffing violently.

'Oh, Bob, you naughty dog,' exclaimed our conductress. 'Don't mind him, sir. He won't do you no harm.'

Bob, indeed, having discovered the intruders, completely changed his manner. He fussed and introduced himself to us in an agreeable manner. [...] Bob was now investigating the legs of Poirot's trousers. Having learned all he could he gave vent to a prolonged sniff ('H'm, not too bad, but not really a doggy person') and returned to me, cocking his head on one side and looking at me expectantly.

16 September

The Secret History, American author Donna Tartt's bestselling debut novel, was first published on this day in 1992. To mark the occasion, our dog today is Frost the greyhound, who makes a brief but heartwarming appearance in the book's pages.

> [Charles and I] drove to Bennington, Manchester, the greyhound track in Pownal, where he ended up bringing home a dog too old to race, in order to save if from being put to sleep. The dog's name was Frost. It loved Camilla, and followed her everywhere: Henry quoted long passages about Emma Bovary and her greyhound.

17 September

American writer Robert B Parker was born on this day in 1932. His *Spenser* series of private detective novels featured a dog named Pearl – and Parker himself owned a German shorthaired pointer of the same name.

> It took Pearl maybe fifteen minutes to calm down, climb up into the white satin armchair in Susan's living room, turn around three times, and lie with her head on her back legs in a tight ball and watch us drink beer.
>
> 'I recall,' Paul said to Susan, 'that you used to kick me off that chair. It was for looking at, not sitting in, you said.'
>
> 'Well, she likes it,' Susan said.

18 September

Half an hour later, Joan glanced over the moribund cactuses in the sun-porch window and saw a raincoated, hatless man, with a head like a polished globe of copper, optimistically ringing at the front door of her neighbour's beautiful brick house. The old Scotty stood beside him in much the same candid attitude as he. Miss Dingwall came out with a mop, let the slowpoke, dignified dog in, and directed Pnin to the Clements' clapboard residence.

– Vladimir Nabokov, *Pnin*

19 September

Today's dog is Patrasche from the 1872 book *A Dog of Flanders* by Marie Louise de la Ramée (who used the pen name Ouida). The novel tells the story of Nello, an orphaned boy growing up near Antwerp, struggling to survive with the help of his ageing grandfather and loyal dog.

For Patrasche was their alpha and omega; their treasury and granary; their store of gold and wand of wealth; their bread-winner and minister; their only friend and comforter. [...] A dog of Flanders – yellow of hide, large of head and limb, with wolf-like ears that stood erect, and legs bowed and feet widened in the muscular development wrought in his breed by many generations of hard service.

20 September

American author George R R Martin was born on this day in 1948. In his honour, today's canines are the direwolves from his epic fantasy novel series *A Song of Ice and Fire*. While out riding one day, a group from Winterfell come across a dead direwolf, even though none have been spotted south of the Wall that separates their country from the icy wilderness beyond for centuries. They realize she has left behind a litter of puppies, and the Stark siblings decide to take one each to raise.

> 'You must train them as well,' their father said. '*You* must train them. The kennelmaster will have nothing to do with these monsters, I promise you that. And the gods help you if you neglect them, or brutalise them, or train them badly. These are not dogs to beg for treats and slink off at a kick. A direwolf will rip a man's arm off his shoulder as easily as a dog will kill a rat. Are you sure you want this?'

21 September

American author and King of Horror Stephen King was born on this day in 1947. Although we've already met one of his dogs this month (8 September), our pooch today is a little less scary: Marlowe, a Welsh corgi gifted to King by his wife Tabitha. Marlowe was famously photographed sitting under King's desk while he worked in 1995. After Marlowe, King got a second corgi, this time named Molly – although he typically refers to her in interviews and online as 'The Thing of Evil'.

22 September

> As I was walking up the stairs, I ran into old Salamano, a neighbour who lives on the same floor as me. He was with his dog. He's had him for eight years and they're always together. The spaniel has a skin disease – mange, I think it's called – which makes him lose almost all his hair and leaves him covered in reddish patches and brown scabs. Because they've lived alone together for so long in one little room, old Salamano has ended up looking like his dog. He also has reddish scabs on his face and yellowish, thinning hair. As for the dog, he's taken on some of his owner's characteristics: hunched up, with his muzzle sticking out and his neck tensed. They look like they're related and yet they hate each other.
>
> – Albert Camus, *The Outsider*

23 September

English novelist Wilkie Collins (author of *The Woman in White*) died on this day in 1889. In his honour, today's dog is Tommie, his beloved Scottish terrier who was frequently mentioned in his letters and even appeared in his 1878 novella *My Lady's Money.*

'I was wondering,' [Felix] began, 'why I miss something when I look round this beautiful room; something familiar, you know, that I fully expected to find here.'

'Tommie?' suggested Lady Lydiard, still watching her nephew as maliciously as ever.

'That's it!' cried Felix, seizing his excuse, and rallying his spirits. 'Why don't I hear Tommie snarling behind me; why don't I feel Tommie's teeth in my trousers?'

The smile vanished from Lady Lydiard's face; the tone taken by her nephew in speaking of her dog was disrespectful in the extreme. She showed him plainly that she disapproved of it. Felix went on, nevertheless, impenetrable to reproof of the silent sort. 'Dear little Tommie! So delightfully fat; and such an infernal temper! I don't know whether I hate him or love him. Where is he?'

24 SEPTEMBER

American writer F Scott Fitzgerald was born on this day in 1896. To mark the occasion, today's dog comes from his iconic 1925 novel *The Great Gatsby.*

'I want to get one of those dogs,' [Mrs Wilson] said earnestly. 'I want to get one for the apartment. They're nice to have – a dog.'

We backed up to a grey old man who bore an absurd resemblance to John D. Rockefeller. In a basket swung from his neck cowered a dozen very recent puppies of an indeterminate breed.

'What kind are they?' asked Mrs Wilson eagerly, as he came to the taxi-window.

'All kinds. What kind do you want, lady?'

'I'd like to get one of those police dogs; I don't suppose you got that kind?'

The man peered doubtfully into the basket, plunged in his hand and drew one up, wriggling, by the back of the neck.

'That's no police dog,' said Tom.

'No, it's not exactly a police dog,' said the man with disappointment in his voice. 'It's more of an Airedale.'

– F. Scott Fitzgerald, *The Great Gatsby*

25 September

American writer William Faulkner was born on this day in 1897. In his honour, today's dog is Lion, the enormous hound from his short story 'The Bear'.

It stood, and they could see it now – part mastiff, something of Airedale and something of a dozen other strains probably, better than thirty inches at the shoulders and weighing as they guessed almost ninety pounds, with cold yellow eyes and a tremendous chest and over all that strange colour like a blued gun barrel.

26 September

We met at Gunter's in Berkeley Square. Julia, like most women then, wore a green hat pulled down to her eyes with a diamond arrow in it; she had a small dog under her arm, three-quarters buried in the fur of her coat. She greeted us with an unusual show of interest.

– Evelyn Waugh, *Brideshead Revisited*

27 September

Our dog today is Bongo from the chilling 2019 horror novel *The Twisted Ones* by T Kingfisher (Ursula Vernon). Bongo is the canine companion to Mouse, a woman who must travel to the home of her abusive grandmother to clear it out following the old woman's death. As she sets to work in this house, deep in the woods, Mouse becomes aware that something isn't right.

> Bongo was facing that direction and, when I took a step, he strode out as if we were going for a perfectly normal walk. His ears and tail were still up, though, and I had the impression that he was thinking very hard about something (or more accurately, that his nose was thinking very hard about something. Bongo's nose is far more intelligent than the rest of him, and I believe it uses his brain primarily as a counterweight).

28 September

We met some of Chaucer's dogs back on 15 June – the monk's hunting greyhounds – but today's medieval pooches are a little more sedate. They are the lap dogs (or 'smal houndes') kept by the Prioress in *The Canterbury Tales.*

> She was so charitable and so pitous
> She wolde wepe if that she saugh a mous
> Kaught in a trappe, if it were deed or bledde.
> Of smale houndes hadde she that she fedde
> With rosted flesh, or milk and wastel breed;
> But soore wepte she if oon of hem were deed.

29 September

English writer Elizabeth Gaskell was born on this day in 1810. She is best known for her novels *North and South* and *Cranford,* but our dog today comes from her 1856 short story 'The Poor Clare'. When Bridget Fitzgerald's beloved spaniel Mignon is deliberately shot by a cruel man during a hunting party, Bridget takes revenge in impressive style, calling down a curse on the man to ensure that the creature he loves best will become plagued by demonic horror.

> She took Mignon up in her arms, and looked hard at the wound; the poor dog looked at her with his glazing eyes, and tried to wag his tail and lick her hand, all covered with blood.

30 September

[J]ust as he arrived by the garden gate he saw a cat inside, going into various arched shapes and fiendish convulsions at the sight of his dog George. The dog took no notice, for he had arrived at an age at which all superfluous barking was cynically avoided as a waste of breath – in fact, he never barked even at the sheep except to order, when it was done with an absolutely neutral countenance, as a sort of Commination-service which, though offensive, had to be gone through once now and then to frighten the flock for their own good.

– Thomas Hardy, *Far From the Madding Crowd*

OCTOBER

Nights are getting longer, the weather's getting cooler and the leaves are starting to change colour and fall. It's a time for crisp autumn walks and cosy cups of tea – always made better with the company of a dog. This month we have two very old texts on the virtues of the canine (6 and 26 October), along with one dog that's actually a metaphor (4 October), one that's a skeleton (29 October) and two who can talk (17 and 25 October).

Of course, October is the month of Halloween, and so in the next chapter, the horrors abound. Spooky dogs to haunt your nightmares can be found on 10, 11, 13 and (naturally) 31 October.

Sleep tight …

1 October

The first serial of Charles Dickens's *Dombey and Son* was published on this day in 1846. Today's dog, then, is the delightful Diogenes, companion to first Paul and then Florence Dombey.

> But though Diogenes was as ridiculous a dog as one would meet with on a summer's day; a blundering, ill-favoured, clumsy, bullet-headed dog, continually acting on a wrong idea that there was an enemy in the neighbourhood, whom it was meritorious to bark at; and though he was far from good-tempered, and certainly was not clever, and had hair all over his eyes, and a comic nose, and an inconsistent tail, and a gruff voice; he was dearer to Florence, in virtue of that parting remembrance of him and that request that he might be taken care of, than the most valuable and beautiful of his kind. So dear, indeed, was this same ugly Diogenes, and so welcome to her, that she took the jewelled hand of Mr Toots and kissed it in her gratitude.

2 October

As we move into October, it makes sense for today's dog to be taken from Roger Zelazny's 1993 novel *A Night in the Lonesome October*. The book is narrated by Snuff the dog, companion to notorious murderer Jack the Ripper, and features cameos from archetypes representing Victor Frankenstein, Sherlock Holmes and Count Dracula.

> I am a watchdog. My name is Snuff. I live with my master Jack outside of London now. I like Soho very much at night with its smelly fogs and dark streets. It is silent then and we go for long walks. Jack is under a curse from long ago and must do much of his work at night to keep worse things from happening. I keep watch while he is about it. If someone comes, I howl.

3 October

English writer and veterinary surgeon James Herriot was born on this day in 1916, and is best known for his series of books about practising as a vet in the Yorkshire Dales in the 1930s–50s. Our dog today is Gyp, the almost-silent sheepdog from his children's book *Only One Woof.*

He was always glad to see me, full of fun, bright-eyed and affectionate. But soundless.

4 October

Today's dog is not really a dog at all. In William Thackeray's *Vanity Fair*, Becky Sharp announces that she needs a 'sheep-dog', but she means a female companion, an older woman to act as her chaperone and make her seem respectable.

'Rawdon,' said Becky, very late one night, as a party of gentlemen were seated round her crackling drawing-room fire (for the men came to her house to finish the night; and she had ice and coffee for them, the best in London): 'I must have a sheep-dog.'

'A what?' said Rawdon, looking up from an *écarté* table.

'A sheep-dog!' said young Lord Southdown. 'My dear Mrs Crawley, what a fancy. Why not have a Danish dog? I know of one as big as a camel-leopard, by Jove. It would almost pull your Brougham. Or a Persian grey-hound, eh? (I propose, if you please); or a little pug that would go in one of Lord Steyne's snuff-boxes? There's a man at Bayswater got one with such a nose that you might – I mark the king and play – that you might hang your hat on it.'

'I mark the trick,' Rawdon gravely said. He attended to his game commonly, and didn't much meddle with the conversation except when it was about horses and betting.

'What *can* you want with a shepherd's dog?' the lively little Southdown continued.

'I mean a *moral* shepherd's dog,' said Becky, laughing, and looking up at Lord Steyne.

'What the devil's that?' said his Lordship.

'A dog to keep the wolves off me,' Rebecca continued. 'A companion.'

5 October

English author, poet and playwright Michael Morpurgo was born on this day in 1943. Today's canine is the biggest fox cub from his 1984 children's novel *Little Foxes.*

It was the largest of the cubs with a redder face than the others and more sharply defined black streaks running from the eyes to the muzzle. The eyes were grey and the nose that pointed at him earth brown. The fox cub sat down neatly and yawned, and Billy found himself yawning in sympathy, a long yawn that lifted the shroud of despondency from Billy's shoulders and left him smiling and happy once again in his Wilderness.

6 October

English scholar, physician and writer John Caius was born on this day in 1510. His works included his 1576 book *Of English Dogges, the Diversities, the Names, the Natures and the Properties.* A publisher's note in the 1880 edition describes it as the earliest book on dogs in the English language.

> I wyll expresse and declare in due order, the grand and generall kinde of English Dogges, the difference of them, the use, the propertyes and the diverse natures of the same, making a tripartite division in this sort and maner.
>
> All English Dogges be eyther of:
> A gentle kinde, serving the game.
> A homely kind, apt for sundry necessary uses.
> A currishe kinde, meete for many toyes.

7 October

William Faulkner's *The Sound and the Fury* was published on this day in 1929. To mark the occasion, today's dog is Blue.

> Dilsey moaned, and when it got to the place I began to cry and Blue howled under the steps. Luster, Frony said in the window, Take them down to the barn. I can't get no cooking done with all that racket. That hound too. Get them outen here.

8 October

In Edgar Allan Poe's *The Narrative of Arthur Gordon Pym of Nantucket,* the narrator stows away on board a whaling vessel, smuggling his pet dog Tiger on board too. While holed away in his hiding place, he falls into a deep sleep, and has a vivid dream in which a lion is about to pounce on him.

> Stifling in a paroxysm of terror, I at last found myself partially awake. My dream, then, was not all a dream. Now, at least, I was in possession of my senses. The paws of some huge and real monster were pressing heavily on my bosom – his hot breath was in my ear – and his white and ghastly fangs were gleaming upon me through the gloom. [...] I felt that my powers of body and mind were fast leaving me – in a word, that I was perishing, and perishing of sheer fright. My brain swam – I grew deadly sick – my vision failed – even the glaring eyeballs above me grew dim. Making a last strong effort, I at length breathed a faint ejaculation to God, and resigned myself to die. The sound of my voice seemed to arouse all the latent fury of the animal. He precipitated himself at full length upon my body; but what was my astonishment when, with a long and low whine, he commenced licking my face and hands with the greatest eagerness, and with the most extravagant demonstration of affection and joy! I was bewildered, utterly lost in amazement – but I could not forget the peculiar whine of my Newfoundland dog Tiger, and the odd manner of his caresses I well knew. It was he.

9 October

> Please may I come in? I am Boots. I am son of Kildonan Brogue – Champion Reserve – V H C – very fine dog; and no-dash-parlour-tricks, Master says, except I can sit-up, and put paws over nose. It is called 'Making Beseech'. Look! I do it out of own head. *Not* for telling … This is Flat-in-Town. I live here with Own God.
>
> – Rudyard Kipling (writing as Boots), *Thy Servant a Dog*

10 October

Susan Hill's gothic horror novel *The Woman in Black* was first published on this day in 1983. In the years since, it has become one of the most iconic ghost stories of our time, spawning a hugely successful stage play and film series. Today's dog is Spider, the sweet-natured terrier loaned to Arthur Kipps by the kind Samuel Daily when Arthur sets out to stay at the eerie Eel Marsh House.

> The little dog Spider had, somewhat to my surprise, slept motionlessly at the foot of my bed. I had taken to her, though I knew little of the way of dogs. She was spirited, lively and alert and yet completely biddable, the expression in her bright eyes, fringed a little by shaggy hair that formed itself somewhat comically into the shape of beetling eyebrows, seemed to me highly intelligent. I thought I was going to be very glad of her.

11 October

From one haunted house to another. Today's 'dog' is the phantom creature that lures Dr Montague and Luke out of the house one night in Shirley Jackson's truly chilling tale *The Haunting of Hill House.*

'We were chasing a dog,' Luke said. 'At least, some animal like a dog.' He stopped, and then went on reluctantly. 'We followed it outside.'

Theodora stared, and Eleanor said, 'You mean it was *inside?*'

'I saw it run past my door,' the doctor said, 'just caught a glimpse of it, slipping along. I woke Luke and we followed it down the stairs and out into the garden and lost it somewhere back of the house.'

'The front door was open?'

'No,' Luke said. 'The front door was closed. So were all the other doors. I checked.'

12 October

The funny thing about Barbara is she has a little dog whom she insists is a well-behaved dog but who, in reality, either barks or tries to bite pretty much everyone who comes near – except Barbara.

– Zadie Smith, 'A Woman with a Little Dog'

13 October

Our dog today is Black Shuck, the legendary ghost dog of English folklore. Said to roam throughout East Anglia, Black Shuck is a large, shaggy black hound who strikes fear into the hearts of all who see him. One such sighting occurred in 1577 in Bungay, Suffolk, and was recorded by Abraham Fleming in an account titled 'A strange and terrible wunder'.

> Immediatly héerupō, there appéered in a moste horrible similitude and likenesse to the congregation then & there present, a dog as they might discerne it, of a black colour: at the sight wherof, togither with the fearful flashes of fire which then were séene, moued such admiration in the mindes of the assemblie, that they thought doomes day was already come. This black dog, or the diuel in such a likenesse (God hée knoweth al who worketh all) runing all along down the body of the Church with great swiftnesse, and incredible haste, among the people, in a visible fourm and shape, passed betwéen two persons, as they were knéeling vppon their knées, and occupied in prayer as it séemed, wrung the necks of them bothe at one instant clene backward, in somuch that euen at a momēt where they kneeled, they strāgely dyed.

14 October

New Zealand author Katherine Mansfield was born on this day in 1888. Our dog today is Lino, who appears in her modernist short story 'A Man and His Dog', alongside his timid-seeming master, Mr Potts.

> In the moment's pause that followed while Lino and his master looked at each other it was curious how strong a resemblance was between them. Then Potts turned again and made for home.
>
> And timidly, as though falling over his own paws, Lino followed after the humble little figure of his master.

15 October

English writer and humourist P G Wodehouse was born on this day in 1881. We met one of his fictional dogs back on 25 August, but today's pups are his real-life Pekinese companions Winks and Boo. He loved the little scamps, and wrote about them in letters to his friend William 'Bill' Townend. In one letter of 1935, he noted:

> What asses Pekes are! We took Winky to Paris, leaving Boo, the other Peke, behind. When we brought her back, was there a joyful reunion? No, sir. Each poor fish had completely forgotten the other, and each, seeing a stranger in her home, prepared to fight to the death. They had six fights in the first ten minutes but have now settled down. One of the fights was the funniest thing you ever

saw. I had put my typewriter case down in a corner and Winky was behind it. Boo came up in front and they both reared up on their hind legs and stood with their noses touching, snarling and growling but unable to get at each other. This went on for about five minutes.

16 October

The Lion, the Witch and the Wardrobe by C S Lewis was published on this day in 1950. Although its best-known animal star is undoubtedly the titular big cat, it does feature the odd canine. Our dog today is the wolf Maugrim, captain of the evil White Witch's secret police force.

Edmund stood and waited, his fingers aching with cold and his heart pounding in his chest, and presently the great wolf, Maugrim, the Chief of the Witch's Secret Police, came bounding back and said, 'Come in! Come in! Fortunate favourite of the Queen – or else not so fortunate.'

And Edmund went in, taking great care not to tread on the Wolf's paws.

17 October

American-British author Patrick Ness was born on this day in 1971. Today's dog is Manchee from his 2008 young adult science fiction novel *The Knife of Never Letting Go.* The book tells the story of Manchee's owner Todd, who lives in a world infected by 'Noise germ' that means everyone's thoughts are audible – including those of animals.

Ben's sent me to pick him some swamp apples and he's made me take Manchee with me, even tho we all know Cillian only bought him to stay on Mayor Prentiss's good side and so suddenly here's this brand new dog as a present for my birthday last year when I never said I wanted any dog [...]. [G]uess who has to feed him and train him and wash him and take him for walks and listen to him jabber now he's got old enough for the talking germ to set his mouth moving? Guess who?

'Poo,' Manchee barks quietly to himself. 'Poo, poo, poo.'

'Just have yer stupid poo and quit yapping about it.'

18 October

It was three o'clock in the beautiful breezy autumn day when Mr Casaubon drove off to his Rectory at Lowick, only five miles from Tipton; and Dorothea, who had on her bonnet and shawl, hurried along the shrubbery and across the park that she might wander through the bordering wood with no other visible companionship than that of Monk, the Great St Bernard dog, who always took care of the young ladies in their walks.

– George Eliot, *Middlemarch*

19 October

Charlotte Brontë's *Jane Eyre* was first published on this day in 1847 under the pen name Currer Bell. To mark this momentous occasion, today's dog is Pilot, Mr Rochester's companion, who is present at the very first interaction between Jane and his master. When the dog rushes past her in the woods, Jane imagines it could be the Gytrash, a folkloric hound not dissimilar to the Black Shuck of 13 October.

> [...] I heard a rush under the hedge, and close down by the hazel stems glided a great dog, whose black and white colour made him a distinct object against the trees. It was exactly one mask of Bessie's Gytrash – a lion-like creature with long hair and a huge head: it passed me, however, quietly enough; not staying to look up, with strange pretercanine eyes, in my face, as I half expected it would. The horse followed,—a tall steed, and on its back a rider. The man, the human being, broke the spell at once. [...] He passed, and I went on: a few steps, and I turned: a sliding sound and an exclamation of 'What the deuce is to do now?' and a clattering tumble, arrested my attention. Man and horse were down; they had slipped on the sheet of ice that glazed the causeway. The dog came bounding back, and seeing his master in a predicament, and hearing the horse groan, barked till the evening hills echoed with the sound, which was deep in proportion to his magnitude. He snuffed around the prostrate group, and then he ran up to me; it was all he could do,—there was no other help to summon. I obeyed him, and walked down to the traveller, by this

time struggling himself free of his steed. His efforts were so vigorous I thought he could not be much hurt; but I asked him the question:— 'Are you injured, sir?'

20 October

Farmer Giles of Ham, J R R Tolkien's comic fable, was published on this day in 1949. Today's dog is Garm, the talking dog owned by Giles.

Farmer Giles had a dog. The dog's name was Garm. Dogs had to be content with short names in the vernacular: the Book-latin was reserved for their betters. Garm could not talk even dog-latin; but he could use the vulgar tongue (as could most dogs of his day) either to bully or brag or to wheedle in. Bullying was for beggars and trespassers, bragging for other dogs, and wheedling for his master. Garm was both proud and afraid of Giles, who could bully and brag better than he could.

21 October

Katherine Paterson's children's novel *The Bridge to Terabithia* was first published on this day in 1977. The book follows the adventures of two children, Jess and Leslie, who create an imaginary kingdom called Terabithia, which they reach by swinging over a creek using a rope swing. Today's dog is Prince Terrien, a puppy that Jess gives Leslie for Christmas. He becomes the guardian and court jester of their magical kingdom.

> Leslie began to laugh. It egged Jess on. Everything the dog did, he imitated, flopping down at last with his tongue lolling out. Leslie was laughing so hard she had trouble getting the words out. 'You— you're crazy. How will we teach him to be a noble guardian. You're turning him into a clown.'
>
> 'R-r-r-roof,' wailed Prince Terrien, rolling his eyes skyward. Jess and Leslie both collapsed. They were in pain from the laughter.
>
> 'Maybe,' said Leslie at last. 'We'd better make him court jester.'

22 October

Jonathan Swift's 1726 novel *Gulliver's Travels* sees the eponymous hero travel to many strange and distant lands, including Lilliput, where the citizens are tiny, and Brobdingnag, where Gulliver himself is the tiny one – and finds himself at the mercy of a curious pooch.

> [A] white spaniel belonging to one of the chief Gardiners, having got by Accident into the Garden, happened to range near the Place where I lay. The Dog following the Scent, came directly up, and taking me in his mouth, ran straight to his Master, wagging his Tail, and set me gently on the ground. By good Fortune he had been so well taught, that I was carried between his Teeth without the least Hurt, or even tearing my cloaths. But, the poor Gardiner, who knew me well, and had a great Kindness for me, was in a terrible Fright.

23 October

Today's dog is Einstein, the genetically enhanced and highly intelligent golden retriever from Dean Koontz's 1987 novel *Watchers.* Koontz is a known dog-lover, and had a golden retriever of his own called Trixie, under whose name he wrote a book entitled *Life is Good: Lessons in Joyful Living.*

Nora held up a flashcard with TREE printed on it. The retriever went unerringly to the photo of the pine tree and indicated it with a touch of his nose. When she held up a card that said CAR, he put a paw on the photo of the car, and when she held up HOUSE, he sniffed at the picture of a colonial mansion. They went through fifty words, and for the first time the dog correctly paired every printed word with the image it represented. Nora was thrilled by his progress, and Einstein could not stop wagging his tail.

Travis said, 'Well, Einstein, you're still a hell of a long way from reading Proust.'

24 October

William Shakespeare's *The Taming of the Shrew* opens with a lord and his huntsman discussing which of their hunting dogs has performed best.

Lord: Huntsman, I charge thee, tender well my hounds.
Breathe Merriman – the poor cur is emboss'd –
And couple Clowder with the deep-mouth'd brach.
Saw'st thou not, boy, how Silver made it good
At the hedge corner, in the coldest fault?
I would not lose the dog for twenty pound.

First Huntsman: Why, Belman is as good as he, my lord;
He cried upon it at the merest loss,
And twice today pick'd out the dullest scent.
Trust me, I take him for the better dog.

Lord: Thou art a fool. If Echo were as fleet,
I would esteem him worth a dozen such.
But sup them well, and look unto them all:
Tomorrow I intend to hunt again.

25 October

Hugh Lofting's children's novel *The Story of Dr Dolittle* was first published this day in 1920. It tells the story of a veterinary surgeon who has learned the skill of speaking to animals.

Today's dog is Jip, one of the doctor's many animal pals.

Jip, who was lying near taking a nap in the sun, began to growl and talk in his sleep.

'I smell roast beef cooking,' he mumbled, 'underdone roast beef – with brown gravy over it.'

'Good gracious!' cried the Doctor. 'What's the matter with the dog? Is he *smelling* in his sleep – as well as talking?'

'I suppose he is,' said Dab-Dab. 'All dogs can smell in their sleep.'

26 October

Only dogs know their master and recognise a stranger if he arrives unexpectedly. They alone recognise their own names and the voice of members of the family. Dogs remember the way to places, however far away, and no animal has a better memory, except man.

– Pliny the Elder, *Natural History: A Selection*

27 OCTOBER

Welsh poet and writer Dylan Thomas was born on this day in 1914. In his honour, please enjoy these few lines from his poem 'The Song of the Mischievous Dog'.

There are many who say that a dog has its day,
And a cat has a number of lives;
There are others who think that a lobster is pink,
And that bees never work in their hives.
There are fewer, of course, who insist that a horse

28 OCTOBER

English writer Evelyn Waugh was born on this day in 1903. His 1948 novel *The Loved One* explores the funeral industry of Los Angeles – including a cemetery just for pets, known as the Happier Hunting Ground.

There was a funeral with full honours that morning, the first for a month. In the presence of a dozen mourners, an Alsatian was lowered into the flower-lined tomb. The Reverend Errol Bartholomew read the service.

'Dog that is born of bitch hath but a short time to live, and is full of misery. He cometh up, and is cut down like a flower; he fleeth as it were a shadow, and never continueth in one stay ...'

29 October

As we approach Halloween, it feels only right that today's dog is the adorable yet bony skeleton dog from Janet and Allan Ahlberg's *Funnybones.* They wrote and illustrated a series of books featuring the big skeleton, the little skeleton and their skeleton dog and cat, and these were later turned into a television series.

30 October

Jane Austen's *Sense and Sensibility* was first published on this day in 1811. Today's dog is Folly, the favourite hound of Sir John Middleton. In the scene quoted below, Sir John is furious to learn of the dastardly Willougby's true nature, as he'd previously promised him one of Folly's puppies.

> Sir John could not have thought it possible. 'A man of whom he had always had such reason to think well! Such a good-natured fellow! He did not believe there was a bolder rider in England! It was an unaccountable business. He wished him at the devil with all his heart. He would not speak another word to him, meet him where he might, for all the world! No, not if it were to be by the side of Barton covert, and they were kept waiting for two hours together. Such a scoundrel of a fellow! such a deceitful dog! It was only the last time they met that he had offered him one of Folly's puppies! and this was the end of it!'

31 October

Today is Halloween, so let's enjoy some of the scariest hounds in literature: the wolves of Bram Stoker's *Dracula,* creatures the Count refers to as 'the children of the night'.

At last there came a time when the driver went further afield than he had yet gone, and in his absence, the horses began to tremble worse than ever and to snort and scream with fright. I could not see any cause for it, for the howling of the wolves had ceased altogether; but just then the moon, sailing through the black clouds, appeared behind the jagged crest of a beetling, pine-clad rock, and by its light I saw around us a ring of wolves, with white teeth and lolling red tongues, with long, sinewy limbs and shaggy hair. They were a hundred times more terrible in the grim silence which held them than even when they howled. For myself, I felt a sort of paralysis of fear. It is only when a man feels himself face to face with such horrors that he can understand their true import.

All at once, the wolves began to howl as though the moonlight had had some peculiar effect on them.

NOVEMBER

Winter is officially upon us, and as tempting as it can be to hibernate indoors, dogs remind us that getting out into the fresh air for a quick stomp around the park can work wonders for our mood in this grey and gloomy month. And once you get back, you can reward yourself by curling up with a snug blanket, a big book and an even bigger cup of tea. This month we'll meet loyal Scotties (29 November), playful spaniels (28 November) and a much-loved Skye terrier (13 November). We'll also get to know a dog who can talk (9 November), and another who is used to space travel (11 November) – along with one of the best-known babysitters in literature (1 November).

1 November

Today's dog is Nana, the delightful and dedicated nursemaid Newfoundland from J M Barrie's *Peter Pan.*

[Their] nurse was a prim Newfoundland dog, called Nana, who had belonged to no one in particular until the Darlings engaged her. She had always thought children important, however, and the Darlings had become acquainted with her in Kensington Gardens, where she spent most of her time peeping into perambulators, and was much hated by careless nursemaids, whom she followed to their homes and complained of to their mistresses. She proved to be quite a treasure of a nurse. How thorough she was at bath-time, and up at any moment of the night if one of her charges made the slightest cry. [...] It was a lesson in propriety to see her escorting her children to school, walking sedately by their side when they were well behaved, and butting them back into line if they strayed. On John's [football] days she never once forgot his sweater, and she usually carried an umbrella in her mouth in case of rain.

2 November

You see, I am a dog – not a scoundrel, a cad, a rascal – no, not a dog in that sense, but an actual dog. *Canis familiaris.* One of the most familiar and loveable (I only repeat the general perception): a Labrador retriever. [...] I am also sentient. I can think. I can remember. [...] Most dogs certainly do not act in ways that would suggest sentience (though I might also add that most humans do not either as is apparent from the hastiest of glances at the newspapers.

– J F Englert, *A Dog About Town*

3 November

Our pups today come from P D Eastman's 1961 early reader book *Go, Dog Go!*, an iconic picture book depicting pooches of all kinds making use of different modes of transport, including bikes, cars, scooters and even a blimp.

4 November

British writer J R Ackerley was born on this day in 1896. Today's dog is his beloved Alsatian Queenie, who appeared under a different name in his 1956 memoir *My Dog Tulip* (14 April) and also in his 1960 novel *We Think the World of You.* In a 1955 letter to artist Lucian Freud, Ackerley wrote:

I hope Queenie will not baffle you. Her invariable behaviour towards visitors will have advantages, I hope, as well as disadvantages. She will expostulate when you enter my sitting-room, in which she lives and sleeps, and will then place herself on the divan bed, on the other side of the room from the window (north light) to guard her biscuits which it is her habit to collect herself. If you are content to sit by the window and draw her she will present a fairly steady picture, I think, staring watchfully at you. But if you are a mover about, I'm afraid she will be noisy. It is her ineducable way. But she does not bite people – at least she has never done so in ten years; she only speaks her mind, rather deafeningly, I fear.

5 November

Our dog today is Ginger Pye, from Eleanor Estes's 1951 book of the same name. It tells the story of a young boy called Jerry Pye, who along with his siblings buys a new puppy they call Ginger.

So Mrs Speedy took the dollar and Jerry tenderly picked up his puppy, his own puppy, his little brown-and-white dog. The children were beside themselves with joy. Here they had this real live puppy, it was theirs, their very own real, honest-to-goodness dog, and nobody else's.

6 November

> Directly he arrived the Count had his books and weapons at hand; his eyes rested upon his favourite pictures; in the hall he was welcomed by his dogs, whose caresses he loved, and his birds, in whose songs he rejoiced; throughout the whole house, suddenly awakened from its long sleep like the Sleeping Beauty's castle in the wood, there burst forth life, song and gaiety.
>
> – Alexandre Dumas, *The Count of Monte Cristo*

7 November

Today's dogs are Jip and Jess, companions of protagonist Griz in C A Fletcher's post-apocalyptic novel *A Boy and His Dog at the End of the World.* Griz, his family and his dogs live on a remote Scottish island, doing their best to survive. When Jess is stolen, Griz and Jip set out on a perilous journey to rescue her.

> Of all the animals that travelled the long road through the ages with us, dogs always walked closest.
>
> And those that remain are still with us now, here at the end of the world. And there may be no law left except what you make it, but if you steal my dog, you can at least expect me to come after you. If we're not loyal to the things we love, what's the point?

8 November

British writer Rumer Godden died on this day in 1998. She was an avowed dog-lover, and canine characters recur throughout her work, including in her 1939 novel *Black Narcissus.*

> This was the time that she used to walk on the shore at Liniskelly or, if the men were coming home early, on the lawn, or go through the fields with the dogs. In the greyness the waves lapped the shore and the boats were getting ready to go out; in the fields the dogs ran on, the chestnut sweep of the setter Roderick's tail busy among the rabbit warrens, Gamble and Morna, the springers, breaking the bracken.

9 November

Today's dog is Sirius, eponymous star of Olaf Stapledon's 1944 science-fiction novel. Sirius is a sheepdog raised by a scientist who has been attempting to hormonally alter dogs to enhance their intelligence. Sirius is born at the same time as the scientist's daughter Plaxy, and the two are raised alongside each other as siblings, with the puppy demonstrating remarkable intelligence and even learning to speak.

> Plaxy was the first to show signs of understanding speech, but Sirius was not far behind. When she began to talk, he often made peculiar little noises which, it seemed, were meant to be imitations of human words. His failure to make himself understood often caused him bitter distress.

He would stand with his tail between his legs miserably whining. Plaxy was the first to interpret his desperate efforts at communication, but Elizabeth in time found herself understanding; and little by little she grew able to equate each of the puppy's grunts and whines with some particular elementary sound of human speech.

10 November

D H Lawrence's novel *Lady Chatterley's Lover* was finally published in full in the UK on this day in 1960, thirty years after the author's death. Having been banned for obscenity for decades, the book's publication caused quite a stir. Today's dog is the canine companion of Oliver Mellors, the gamekeeper (and titular lover). Ever-present, the sweet-natured brown spaniel seems to herald the arrival of her taciturn master.

She was watching a brown spaniel that had run out of a side-path and was looking towards them with a lifted nose, making a soft, fluffy bark. A man with a gun strode swiftly, softly, out after the dog, facing their way as if to attack them; then stopped instead, saluted, and was turning downhill. It was only the new game-keeper, but he had frightened Connie, he seemed to emerge with such a swift menace.

11 November

American writer Kurt Vonnegut was born on this day in 1922. Although best known for his bestselling and critically acclaimed 1969 novel *Slaughterhouse-Five*, our dog today is the space-travelling Kazak, who appears (and materializes) in his 1959 science-fiction work *The Sirens of Titan*.

> Somewhere on the estate a mastiff bayed. The baying sounded like the blows of a maul on a great bronze gong.
>
> Constant awoke from his contemplation of the fountain. The baying could only be that of Kazak, the hound of space. Kazak had materialised. Kazak smelled the blood of a parvenu.
>
> Constant sprinted the remainder of the distance to the house.

12 November

Children's novel *The Sheep-Pig* by Dick King-Smith was first published on this day in 1983, later inspiring the hit 1995 film *Babe*. The book tells the story of a piglet who is separated from his family and moved to a new farm, where the sheepdog Fly takes him under her paw and begins to teach him how to herd sheep. Although by the end of the book, Babe the pig is an honorary dog, today we are celebrating Fly herself.

> As soon as Fly moved the piglet woke and followed her, sticking so close to her that his snout touched her tail-tip. Surprise forced Farmer Hogget into speech.

'Fly!' he said in astonishment. Obediently as always, the collie bitch turned and trotted back to him. The pig trotted behind her.

'Sit!' said Farmer Hogget. Fly sat. Babe sat. Farmer Hogget scratched his head. He could not think of anything to say.

13 November

Scottish novelist and poet Robert Louis Stevenson was born on this day in 1850. He is best known for his novels *Treasure Island* and *The Strange Case of Dr Jekyll and Mr Hyde*. As a child, he had a beloved Skye terrier named Cuillin, who has been immortalized in bronze as part of a statue depicting a young Stevenson writing in a notebook and petting his dog. The statue stands in a garden outside Colinton Parish Church in Edinburgh, Scotland.

14 November

He had the kind of legs that go round in circles. He orbited me. He was a universe of play. Why did I walk so purposefully in a straight line? Where would it take me? He went round and round and we got there all the same.

– Jeanette Winterson, 'The Twenty-four Hour Dog'

15 November

English writer Richmal Crompton was born on this day in 1890. In her honour, today's dog is Jumble from her hilarious *Just William* books.

> 'Hey, Jumble!' [William] called.
>
> After all, life could never be absolutely black, as long as it held Jumble.
>
> Jumble darted ecstatically from the kitchen regions, his mouth covered with gravy, dropping a half-picked bone on the hall carpet as he came.

16 November

> The little dogs and all,
> Tray, Blanch and Sweetheart, see, they bark at me.
>
> – William Shakespeare, *King Lear, Act III, Scene VI*

17 November

Our dog today is the wily wolf from the classic children's fairy tale, 'Little Red Riding Hood'. Children all over the world know the story of the little girl who sets out in her red cape to visit her grandmother in the heart of the woods. And children all over the world have struggled to understand how, upon being greeted with a literal wolf wearing her grandmother's clothes, Little Red seems to see very little amiss. Sure, she comments on the size of her grandmother's eyes and teeth, but she doesn't seem to clock that she's speaking to a *wolf*. Still, there are few fairy-tale images more amusing than that of a huge wolf wearing a nightie and a frilly cap.

18 NOVEMBER

Celebrated Canadian writer Margaret Atwood was born on this day in 1939. The extract below comes from her 2000 novel *The Blind Assassin.*

You should get a dog, he says.

She laughs. A dog? Why?

Then you'd have an excuse. You could take it for walks. Me and the dog.

The dog would be jealous of you, she says. And you'd think I liked the dog better.

But you wouldn't like the dog better, he says. Would you?

She opens her eyes wider. Why wouldn't I?

He says, Dogs can't talk.

19 NOVEMBER

Indeed when I reflect on it – and I have time and disposition and capacity enough for that – I see that dogdom is in every way a marvellous institution.

– Franz Kafka, 'Investigations of a Dog'

20 November

Leo Tolstoy died on this day in 1910. We already met one of his canine characters back on 9 September. Today's dog is the bulldog Búlka, about whom he wrote several short stories.

> I had a small bulldog. He was called Búlka. He was black; only the tips of his front feet were white. All bulldogs have their lower jaws longer than the upper, and the upper teeth come down behind the nether teeth, and Búlka's lower jaw protruded so much that I could put my finger between the two rows of teeth. His face was broad, his eyes large, black and sparkling; and his teeth and incisors stood out prominently. [...] He was gentle and did not bite, but he was strong and stubborn. If he took hold of a thing, he clenched his teeth and clung to it like a rag, and it was not possible to tear him off, any more than as though he were a lobster.

21 November

I step through origins
like a dog turning
its memories of wilderness
on the kitchen mat.

– Seamus Heaney, 'Kinship'

22 November

American writer Jack London died on this day in 1916. We first met him back on 12 January. Today's dog is White Fang, star of his 1906 novel of the same name.

> He became quicker of movement than the other dogs, swifter of foot, craftier, deadlier, more lithe, more lean with ironlike muscle and sinew, more enduring, more cruel, more ferocious, and more intelligent. He had to become all these things, else he would not have held his own nor survived the hostile environment in which he found himself.

23 November

English writer and suffragette Clemence Housman was born on this day in 1861. Her 1896 novel *The Were-Wolf* tells the story of a woman named White Fell who arrives at a remote Scandinavian village. She is quickly welcomed by the community, but one man (and one dog) quickly realize that she is not just a woman – she's a werewolf.

> In a horror of surprise, Christian stood dazed a moment: then he lifted the latch and went in. His glance took in all the old familiar forms and faces, and with them that of the stranger, fur-clad and beautiful. The awful truth flashed upon him: he knew what she was.

24 November

Emily Brontë's classic Gothic novel *Wuthering Heights* was first published on this day in 1847 (under the name Ellis Bell). Our dogs today are the hounds kept by Heathcliff, who torment Mr Lockwood when he attempts to steal a lantern in the novel's opening chapters.

He sat within earshot, milking the cows by the light of a lantern, which I seized unceremoniously, and, calling out that I would send it back on the morrow, rushed to the nearest postern.

'Maister, maister, he's staling t' lantern!' shouted the ancient, pursuing my retreat. 'Hey, Gnasher! Hey, dog! Hey, Wolf, holld him, holld him!'

On opening the little door, two hairy monsters flew at my throat, bearing me down, and extinguishing the light; while a mingled guffaw from Heathcliff and Hareton put the copestone on my rage and humiliation. Fortunately, the beasts seemed more bent on stretching their paws, and yawning, and flourishing their tails, than devouring me alive; but they would suffer no resurrection, and I was forced to lie till their malignant masters pleased to deliver me.

25 November

Our dog today is John Joiner, who appears in Beatrix Potter's *The Roly-Poly Pudding*. When young Tom Kitten finds his way into the home of a family of rats living under the floorboards, they set to work turning him into a 'kitten dumpling roly-poly pudding'. Luckily for him, his mother Tabitha Twitchitt has sent for John Joiner, a carpenter dog, who takes up the floorboards and frightens the rats away.

26 November

American cartoonist Charles M Schulz was born on this day in 1922. He is best known for his much-loved *Peanuts* comic strip, starring one of the world's favourite fictional dogs, Snoopy the beagle. Snoopy is said to have been inspired by a dog named Spike that Schulz owned as a child. Snoopy is often seen writing on a typewriter, making him a truly literary pooch.

27 November

Our dog today is Finn, from Charlotte Wood's 2020 novel *The Weekend*. The book depicts three women meeting for a weekend after a friend of theirs, Sylvie, has passed away. One of them, Wendy, has an ageing dog called Finn, whom we learn was gifted to her by Sylvie following her partner's death.

It was seventeen years ago that Sylvie had turned up at Wendy's house, a month after the funeral, with two cardboard boxes. It felt like last week, and a lifetime ago. [...] Sylvie had drawn out the small white bewildered puppy from one of her boxes. She did not try to make Wendy play with it, or want it. She'd put it on the floor and then emptied the other bag: a bag of food, two bowls, a dog bed. [...] Sylvie said, 'Lab-poodle cross, if you can believe that. Designer mutt.'

28 November

Children's writer Enid Blyton died on this day in 1968. We've already met Buster (11 August) and Timmy (11 September), so today's pooch is the adorable Scamper, a golden spaniel and canine star of *The Secret Seven* books.

Peter finished [writing his notes] first. He let Scamper lick the envelopes. He was good at that; he had such a nice big wet tongue.

'You're a very licky dog,' said Peter, 'so you must be pleased when you have things like this to lick. It's a pity we're not putting stamps on the letters, then you could lick those, too.'

'Now, shall we go and deliver the secret messages?' said Janet. 'Mummy said we could go out; it's a nice sunny morning – but won't it be cold!'

'Woof! woof!' said Scamper, running to the door when he heard the word 'out'. He pawed at the door impatiently.

29 November

The Scottie is at heart a gentleman – deep-natured, reserved, honourable, patient, tolerant and courageous. He never whines or complains: he meets life as he finds it, with an instinctive philosophy of stoical intrepidity, and a mellow understanding. He is calm and firm – and stubborn. He minds his own business – and minds it well. [...] You know where you are with a Scottie; and if you are a friend, he is gentle and loving and protective ... And this is the dog, Markham, that certain breeders would turn into a grotesque zany – a butt for humour, an object for snickering – by taking away his beautiful proportions, lengthening his foreface [and] shortening his body and tail.

– S S Van Dine, *The Kennel Murder Case*

30 November

Canadian author L M Montgomery was born on this day in 1874. She is best known for her 1908 novel *Anne of Green Gables,* which sparked a whole series based on the lives of Anne Shirley and those around her. Today's dog is Dog Monday from her 1921 novel *Rilla of Ingleside,* which is focused on Anne's daughter. Dog Monday is owned by Rilla's brothers, but is left behind when the young men of the town set out to fight in the First World War.

> Dog Monday was the Ingleside dog, so called because he had come into the family on a Monday when Walter had been reading *Robinson Crusoe.* He really belonged to Jem but was much attached to Walter also. He was lying beside Walter now with nose snuggled against his arm, thumping his tail rapturously whenever Walter gave him an absent pat. Monday was not a collie or a setter or a hound or a Newfoundland. He was just, as Jem said, 'plain dog' – *very* plain dog, uncharitable people added. [...] Inside his homely hide beat the most affectionate, loyal, faithful heart of any dog since dogs were; and something looked out of his eyes that was nearer akin to a soul than any theologian would allow.

DECEMBER

As the end of the year draws near, December is a time to be with our loved ones, perhaps celebrating Christmas or Hanukkah, enjoying good company, great food and plenty of wintery walks. With that in mind, we'll enjoy a few festive pooches this month (24 and 25 December), as well as meeting a witch's familiar (28 December), a spoilt pug (16 December) and a furry cynic (19 December).

As well as being a time for festivities, December is also a month for reflection and review: a chance to look back over the year that has passed and think about what we've experienced and learned. This month, our dogs teach us some rather valuable lessons, including the importance of appreciating what we have (1 December) and learning how to simply 'be' (10 December).

1 December

Our dog today is the hapless hound who appears in Aesop's fable 'The Dog and his Reflection'. The little dog is pootling along, holding a delicious bone in his mouth, when he crosses a stream and looks down to see another dog looking back up at him. That dog has a bone, too, but he suspects it might be bigger than his own, so he drops his, meaning to take the other dog's bone instead. Of course, it was only his reflection, and now the poor pooch has no bone at all.

2 December

Today's dog is the brave little puppy featured in Julie Myerson's stunning 2016 literary ghost story *The Stopped Heart*. Dogs are often credited with being able to sense the presence of something otherworldly, making them very useful creatures to have around if you find yourself living in a haunted house.

> Mary stands in the kitchen, one hand on the old pine table, holding herself still and watching the space between the chair and the dresser. Air, white-painted wall, skirting board. She can't take her eyes off it, that space. The dog gets up out of her basket and walks towards the same place and, head on one side, stares and begins to growl.
>
> Mary can't help it, she takes a step backwards, away. She looks at the dog.
>
> 'What?' she whispers. 'What is it?'

3 December

> I remembered reading somewhere that a dog ages seven years for each one of ours. Just a rule of thumb, surely, but at least a way to figure, and what did that mean to a dog, time-wise? If I came back at six to feed her, that would be about twelve hours of my time. Would that be eighty-four hours for her? Three and a half days? If so, no wonder she was so happy to see me.
>
> – Stephen King, *Fairy Tale*

4 December

Our dog today is Bob, also known as Bobby, the sweet little pooch who captures the heart of the protagonist of Beth Morrey's 2020 novel *Saving Missy.* The book tells the story of Missy Carmichael, who has resigned herself to a life of anxiety and loneliness, until she finds herself making new friends – and taking in a dog called Bob.

> I slept deeply, and in the morning when I awoke, two things struck me at once. One: Bob was curled at the end of my bed, snoring loudly, hairs all over the covers, the door to my bedroom still closed. And two: for the first time in my life, ever since Fa-Fa told us the story about the ripper who sang nursery rhymes from the wardrobe before he cut up his victims, I hadn't checked the cupboards before I went to sleep.

5 December

Iconic American writer Joan Didion was born on this day in 1934. Celebrated for her thought-provoking, honest and graceful prose, Didion wrote both fiction and non-fiction, and her best-known works include the memoir *The Year of Magical Thinking* and her essay collections *Slouching Towards Bethlehem* and *The White Album*. Today's dog is her soft-coated wheaten terrier, Ellie, who became Didion's companion towards the end of her life.

6 December

Our dog today is the hero and narrator of O Henry's 1906 short story 'Memoirs of a Yellow Dog'. The pooch relates how little he enjoys his mistress's suffocating attentions, and the fact that she calls him 'Lovey', and then describes a moment of somewhat inebriated connection with his master that earns him a new – and much preferred – name.

> But what pleased me most was when my old man pulled both of my ears until I howled and said:
>
> 'You common, monkey-headed, rat-tailed, sulphur-coloured son of a doormat, do you know what I'm going to call you?'
>
> I thought of 'Lovey', and I whined dolefully.
>
> 'I'm going to call you "Pete",' says my master; and if I'd had five tails I couldn't have done enough wagging to do justice to the occasion.

7 December

> His friend, and mine too, was the yard dog Suso. The bearer of this singular name was a rather mangy setter. When one brought her her food she used to grin across her whole face, but she was by no means good-natured to strangers, and led the unnatural life of a dog chained all day to its kennel and only let free to roam the court at night.
>
> – Thomas Mann, *Doctor Faustus*

8 December

English novelist Louis de Bernières was born on this day in 1954. Today's dog is Tally Ho (later just called 'Red Dog'), the star of his 2002 novel *Red Dog*. The book depicts the life of a Red Cloud Kelpie in Western Australia, and was inspired by a statue of a dog the author saw when visiting the region.

> Tally waited until the Land Rover had started off down the road, before springing lightly once more over on to the front passenger seat. He sat down quickly and stuck his head out of the window, into the breeze, so that he would have a good excuse for not hearing his master telling him to get in the back. Jack raised his eyebrows, shook his head and sighed. Tally Ho was an obstinate dog, without a doubt, and didn't consider himself to be anyone's subordinate, not even Jack's. It never occurred to him that he was less than equal, and in that respect you might say he was rather like a cat, although he probably wouldn't have liked the comparison.

9 December

On this day in 1852, Dickens wrote to his editor W H Wills to complain about dogs barking and distracting him from his work.

My dear Wills,

I am driven mad by dogs, who have taken it into their accursed heads to assemble every morning in the piece of ground opposite, and who have barked this morning *for five hours without intermission*; positively rendering it impossible for me to work, and so making what is really ridiculous quite serious to me. I wish, between this and dinner, you would send John to see if he can hire a gun, with a few caps, some powder, and a few charges of small shot. If you duly commission him with a card, he can easily do it. And if I get those implements up here to-night, I'll be the death of some of them to-morrow morning.

10 December

Brazilian writer Clarice Lispector was born on this day in 1920. Today's dog is her beloved companion Ulisses (Ulysses), who appears in her posthumous novel *A Breath of Life*.

My dog reinvigorates me completely. Not to mention that he sometimes falls asleep at my feet filling my bedroom with hot humid life. My dog teaches me to live. All he does is 'be'. 'Being' is his activity. And being is my most profound intimacy. When he falls asleep in my lap I watch over him and his very rhythmical breathing. And – he motionless in my lap – we form a single organic being, a living mute statue. [...] My dog is as dog as a human is human. I love the doggishness and the hot humanity of both.

11 December

Today's dog is Otto, the 'good as gold' German shepherd from Elena Ferrante's 2002 novel *The Days of Abandonment*. The book follows mother-of-two Olga in the days and weeks after her husband announces he is leaving her. Blindsided and confused, Olga's world seems to crumble around her as she adjusts to her new life. Dog-lovers beware – Otto's ending is not a happy one.

> One night I heard a noise in the house, like a piece of paper gliding quickly over the floor, pushed by a current of air.
>
> The dog whined in fear. Otto, although a German shepherd, was not very courageous.

12 December

French novelist Gustave Flaubert was born on this day in 1821. Today's dog is Djali from his celebrated novel *Madame Bovary*. Djali is Emma Bovary's beloved greyhound – and is referenced in *The Secret History*, as we saw on 16 September.

She called Djali, held her between her knees, stroked her long delicate head and told her:

– Come on, kiss missy. Not a care in the world, have you?

Then, gazing at the elegant creature's melancholy expression as it slowly gave a yawn, she was moved; and, comparing it to herself, she spoke aloud to it, as if consoling one of the afflicted.

13 December

Judge: What do you consider sins, Anton Antonovich? There are sins, and sins. I'm not ashamed to say it – I take bribes. But what kind of bribes? Puppies! That's altogether different.
Mayor: Puppies or whatever, a bribe is a bribe.
Judge: I can't go along with that, Anton Antonovich.

– Nikolai Gogol, *The Government Inspector*

14 December

Near the Churchill, now itself peacefully sleeping, I came across an old guy walking a little dog. The dog was frantically trying to pee on every vertical surface and in consequence wasn't so much walking as being dragged along on three legs.

– Bill Bryson, *Notes from a Small Island*

15 December

Our dog today is Rover, from J R R Tolkien's novella *Roverandom.* Rover is an excitable puppy who is turned into a toy by a grumpy wizard, and then embarks on an adventure to try and find someone who can turn him back into a real dog.

When the little boys were asleep, Rover stretched his tired, stiff legs and gave a little bark that nobody heard except an old wicked spider up a corner. Then he jumped from the chair to the bed, and from the bed he tumbled off onto the carpet; and then he ran away out of the room and down the stairs and all over the house.

Although he was very pleased to be able to move again, and having once been real and properly alive he could jump and run a good deal better than most toys at night, he found it very difficult and dangerous getting about. He was now so small that going downstairs was almost like jumping off walls; and getting upstairs again was very tiring and awkward indeed.

16 December

Legendary English novelist Jane Austen was born on this day in 1775. Today's dog is the endlessly spoilt Pug of her 1814 novel *Mansfield Park.*

> To the education of her daughters, Lady Bertram paid not the smallest attention. She had not time for such cares. She was a woman who spent her days in sitting nicely dressed on a sofa, doing some long piece of needle-work, of little use and no beauty, thinking more of her pug than her children, but very indulgent to the latter, when it did not put herself to inconvenience, guided in everything important by Sir Thomas, and in smaller concerns by her sister.

17 December

The long-haired collie Lassie first appeared in a short story written by Eric Knight and published on this day in 1938 in the *Saturday Evening Post*. Knight later expanded the story in to a novel called *Lassie Come-Home,* which was published in 1940, and Lassie went on to become the subject of several films and TV series.

> [Lassie] ran beside him, leaping high in the air, barking that sharp cry of happiness that dogs often can achieve. Her mouth was stretched wide, as collies so frequently do in their glad moments and in a way that makes collie owners swear that their dogs laugh when pleased.

18 December

> Turns out Rebecca's parents' 'country cottage' has stable blocks, outbuildings, pool, full staff and its own church in the 'garden'. As we scrunched across the gravel, Rebecca – snooker-ball-bottomed in jeans in manner of Ralph Lauren ad – was playing with a dog, sunlight dappling her hair, amongst an array of Saab and BMW convertibles.
>
> 'Emma! Get down! Hiiiiii!' she cried, at which dog broke free and put its nose straight up my coat.
>
> 'Mwah' come and have a drink,' she said, welcoming Mark as I wrestled with the dog's head.
>
> – Helen Fielding, *Bridget Jones: The Edge of Reason*

19 December

Today's dog is Happy Dan, the star of writer Ward Green's 1945 short story 'Happy Dan, the Cynical Dog'. The story was read by Walt Disney, and went on to become the inspiration for the character of Tramp in the 1955 cartoon film *Lady and the Tramp.*

> Happy Dan, a spaniel, was not like other dogs. Most dogs believe men are good, cats are evil and birds can be caught by chasing them; they have illusions. Happy Dan was born with practically none, and by the time he was six months old he had lost those. He believed in nothing, not even his master's voice. He was a cynic.

20 December

English writer Kate Atkinson was born on this day in 1951. To mark her birthday, today's dog is Bosun, from her 2013 novel *Life After Life*.

They had a dog. A big, brindled French mastiff called Bosun. 'The name of Byron's dog,' Sylvie said. Ursula had no idea who the mysterious Byron was but he showed no interest in reclaiming his dog from them. Bosun had soft loose furry skin that rolled beneath Ursula's fingers and his breath smelt of the scrag-end that Mrs Glover, to her disgust, had to stew for him. He was a good dog, Hugh said, a responsible dog, the kind that pulled people from burning buildings and rescued them from drowning.

21 December

I opened the book at random, in the manner of a lucky dip. It fell open at a pivotal scene, the one where Jane meets Mr Rochester for the first time, startling his horse in the woods and causing him to fall. Pilot is there too, the handsome, soulful-eyed hound. If the book has one failing, it's that there is insufficient mention of Pilot. You can't have too much dog in a book.

– Gail Honeyman, *Eleanor Oliphant is Completely Fine*

22 December

George Eliot (also known as Mary Ann Evans) died on this day in 1880. In her honour, today's dog is Gyp from her 1859 novel *Adam Bede.* Following the novel's success, Eliot's publisher presented her with a pet pug named, fittingly enough, 'Pug' – the name of one of the other dogs in the book.

> Hitherto, Gyp had kept his comfortable bed, only lifting up his head and watching Adam more closely, as he noticed the other workmen departing. But no sooner did Adam put his ruler in his pocket, and began to twist his apron round his waist, than Gyp ran forward and looked up in his master's face with patient expectation. If Gyp had had a tail he would doubtless have wagged it, but being destitute of that vehicle for his emotions, he was like many other worthy personages, destined to appear more phlegmatic than nature had made him.
>
> 'What, art ready for the basket, eh, Gyp?' said Adam [...].
>
> Gyp jumped and gave a short bark, as much as to say, 'Of course.' Poor fellow, he had not a great range of expression.

23 December

American writer Donna Tartt was born on this day in 1963. To mark the occasion, our pooch today is Popper (sometimes Popchik or Popchyk) from her 2013 novel *The Goldfinch.*

Irritably, with a groan, Popper shifted over to make room. Tiny as he was, and ridiculous-looking, still he was a fierce barker and territorial about his place next to me; and I knew if anyone opened the bedroom door while I was sleeping – even Xandra or my dad, neither of whom he liked much – he would jump up and raise the alarm.

24 December

Tchaikovsky's ballet *The Nutcracker* has become a festive institution, telling the story of a magical nutcracker who comes to life one Christmas Eve and leads an army of gingerbread soldiers in battle against an army of mice, all witnessed by a little girl named (in the ballet) Clara. It is based on E T A Hoffmann's 1816 tale *The Nutcracker and the Mouse King*, in which a young girl called Maria has to sacrifice her toys and sugar figurines (including a sugar dog) to the mice in order to save her treasured nutcracker.

Maria was very sad; she went the next morning to the glass case, and gazed with the most sorrowful looks at her sugar and chocolate figures. And her grief was reasonable, for thou canst not imagine, my attentive reader, what beautiful figures of sugar and chocolate little Maria Stahlbaum possessed. A pretty shepherd and shepherdess watched a whole flock of milk-white lambs, while a little dog frisked about them; next came two letter-carriers, with letters in their hands; and then four neat pairs of nicely dressed boys and girls, with gay ribbons.

25 December

Today is Christmas Day, so it seems fitting that our dog is Max, companion of the foul-tempered Grinch in Dr Seuss's 1957 picture book *How the Grinch Stole Christmas.* When the Grinch hatches his dastardly plan to steal Christmas from the inhabitants of Whoville, he disguises his pet dog Max as a reindeer and makes him pull his sleigh.

26 December

> 'Men,' said Mr Kyle, 'people have been trying to understand dogs since the beginning of time. One never knows what they'll do. You can read every day where a dog saved the life of a drowning child, or lay down his life for his master. Some people call this loyalty. I don't. I may be wrong, but I call it love – the deepest kind of love.'
>
> – Wilson Rawls, *Where the Red Fern Grows*

27 December

Today's dog is technically a ship. On this day in 1831, the HMS *Beagle* set sail from Plymouth on an expedition that would end up lasting almost five years. On board was Charles Darwin, who later recounted his experiences in his 1839 book *The Voyage of the Beagle.* As well as devoting his life to the study of nature and biology, Darwin was an avowed dog-lover, keeping many canine companions throughout his life, including Spark, Polly, Snow and Dash.

28 December

Today's dog is Coal, the black Labrador who serves as Alexandra Spofford's pet and familiar in John Updike's 1984 novel *The Witches of Eastwick.* In the passage below, Alexandra is walking Coal on the beach, resentful that the place is too crowded to allow her to let him off the lead. She has just been heckled by a group of young men as she and her pet walked past.

> Alexandra felt irritated and vengeful. Her insides felt bruised; she resented the overheard insult 'hag' and the general vast insult of all this heedless youth prohibiting her from letting her dog, her friend and familiar, run free. She decided to clear the beach for herself and Coal by willing a thunderstorm.

29 December

Our dog today is Holiday from Alice Sebold's 2002 haunting novel *The Lovely Bones.* The book is narrated by a young girl named Susie Salmon, who has been murdered and is now watching on from the afterlife as investigators attempt to solve her murder. Holiday is the Salmon family pet, and provides much-needed comfort to Susie's siblings and parents following her disappearance.

> I tried to take solace in Holiday, our dog. I missed him in a way I hadn't yet let myself miss my mother and father, my sister and brother. That way of missing would mean that I had accepted that I would never be with them again; it might sound silly but I didn't believe it, would not believe it. Holiday stayed with Lindsey at night, stood by my father each time he answered the door to a new unknown. Gladly partook of any clandestine eating on the part of my mother. Let Buckley pull his tail and ears inside the house of locked doors.

30 December

Sinbad the dog was a non-commissioned officer who died on this day in 1951. He was Chief Dog aboard the USCGC *Campbell* and was immortalized in the book *Sinbad of the Coast Guard.*

31 December

We finish the year with another dog from the world of Sherlock Holmes, but this dog is not sniffing around helping to solve the mystery like Toby (6 January), nor the mysterious beast at the heart of the investigation like the hound of the Baskervilles (25 March). Instead, this dog, which appears in Arthur Conan Doyle's short story 'The Adventure of Silver Blaze', helps to provide the great detective with a clue – by doing precisely nothing. Realizing that the dog did not bark when disturbed, Holmes deduces that the criminal they are seeking must be someone with whom the dog is familiar.

> 'Is there any other point to which you would wish to draw my attention?'
>
> 'To the curious incident of the dog in the night time.'
>
> 'The dog did nothing in the night time.'
>
> 'That was the curious incident,' remarked Sherlock Holmes.

REFERENCES

Ackerley, J. R. *My Dog Tulip*. Poseidon, 1987.
Ackerley, J. R. *The Ackerley Letters*. Edited by Neville Braybrook. Harcourt Brace, 1975.
Adams, Douglas. *So Long, and Thanks for all the Fish*. Pan Books, 2009.
Adams, Douglas. *The Salmon of Doubt: Hitchhiking the Galaxy One Last Time*. Macmillan, 2002.
Adams, Richard. *The Plague Dogs*. Vintage, 2016.
Ahlberg, Allan. *Woof!* Puffin, 1998.
Allende, Isabel. *The House of the Spirits*. Jonathan Cape, 1985.
Andersen, Hans Christian. *The Tinderbox*. Penguin Classics, 2015.
Armstrong, William. *Sounder*. Scholastic, 2003.
Atkinson, Kate. *Life After Life*. Black Swan, 2014.
Atwood, Margaret. *The Blind Assassin*. Anchor, 2001.
Aubry, Cécile. *Belle and Sébastien*. Alma, 2017.
Austen, Jane. *Mansfield Park*. John Murray, 1816.
Austen, Jane. *Northanger Abbey*. Penguin, 2006.
Austen, Jane. *Persuasion*. J. Grant, 1906.
Austen, Jane. *Sense and Sensibility*. Richard Bentley, 1853.
Auster, Paul. *Timbuktu*. H. Holt, 1999.
Awad, Mona. *Bunny*. Head of Zeus, 2019.
Barrett Browning, Elizabeth. Letter to H. S. Boyd, 2 March 1842. *The Letters of Elizabeth Barrett Browning*. Edited by Frederic G. Kenyon. Smith, Elder & Co, 1898.
Barrie, J. M. *Peter Pan*. Create Space, 2015.
Battersby, Eileen. *Ordinary Dogs: A Story of Two Lives*. Faber and Faber, 2012.
Baudelaire, Charles. 'The Dog and the Vial'. *Baudelaire: His Prose and Poetry*. Translated by Thomas Robert Smith. Boni & Liveright, 1919.
Baum, Frank L. *The Road to Oz*. Reilly & Lee, 1909.
Baum, L. Frank. *The Wonderful Wizard of Oz*. Watermill, 1983.
Beaton, M. C. *Death of a Nag*. Robinson, 2009.
Beckett, Samuel. *Malone Dies*. Penguin, 1962.
Beckett, Samuel. *Waiting for Godot*. Faber & Faber, 1956.
Bemelmans, Ludwig. *Madeline's Rescue*. Penguin, 1981.
Blyton, Enid. *Five on a Treasure Island*. Hodder, 2017.
Blyton, Enid. *The Mystery of the Burnt Cottage*. Granada, 1966.
Blyton, Enid. *The Secret Seven & Secret Seven Adventure*. Knight, 1986.
Bonhams. 'A fragment of the original draft of *Of Mice and Men*, eaten by the dog'. Bonhams.com

Brontë, Anne. *The Tenant of Wildfell Hall*. Penguin, 2012.
Brontë, Charlotte. *Jane Eyre*. Harper & Brothers, 1899.
Brontë, Emily. *Wuthering Heights*. Barnes & Noble, 2004.
Brown, John. *Rab and His Friends, and Other Papers*. Frederick A. Stokes, 1893.
Bryson, Bill. *Notes from a Small Island*. Black Swan, 1996.
Bulgakov, Mikhail. *The Master and Margarita*. Grove Press, 1995.
Burnett, Frances Hodgson. *A Little Princess*. Charles Scribner's Sons, 1905.
Burns, Robert. 'The Twa Dogs'. scottishpoetrylibrary.org.
Butcher, Jim. *Dead Beat*. Roc, 2005.
Byron, George Gordon. 'Epitaph to a Dog'. poets.org.
Caius, John. *The Works of John Caius, M. D., Second Founder of Gonville and Caius College and Master of the College, 1559–1573*. Cambridge University Press, 1912.
Cameron, Julia. *Write for Life*. Profile, 2023.
Cameron, W. Bruce. *A Dog's Purpose*. Forge, 2010.
Camus, Albert. *The Outsider*. Penguin, 2013.
Caras, Roger A. *A Celebration of Dogs*. Times Books, 1982.
Carlyle, Jane Welsh. *Jane Welsh Carlyle: Letters to her Family, 1839–63*. John Murray, 1924.
Carroll, Lewis. *Alice's Adventures in Wonderland*. Macmillan, 2025.
Carter, Angela. 'The Company of Wolves'. *The Bloody Chamber*. Penguin, 1993.
Chaucer, Geoffrey. *The Canterbury Tales*. Oxford, 1998.
Chekhov, Anton. 'The Lady with the Dog'. *The Lady with the Dog & Other Stories*. Wiley, 1917.
Christie, Agatha. *Dumb Witness*. William Morrow, 2011.
Christie, Agatha. *The Moving Finger*. Harper Collins, 2005.
Christie's. 'Kerouac's original typescript scroll of *On the Road*'. https://www.christies.com/en/lot/lot-2053069
Clements, Mikaella, and Datta, Onjuli. *Feast While You Can*. Simon & Schuster, 2024.
Colette. *Barks and Purrs*. projectgutenberg.org.
Collodi, Carlo. *The Adventures of Pinocchio*. Grosset & Dunlap, 1946.
Conan Doyle, Arthur. 'The Adventure of Silver Blaze'. *Memoirs of Sherlock Holmes*. Quality Paperback Club, 1994.
Conan Doyle, Arthur. *The Hound of the Baskervilles*. Penguin, 2008.
Conan Doyle, Arthur. *The Sign of the Four*. Filiquarian, 2007.
Cresswell, Helen. *Absolute Zero*. Avon Books, 1985.
Crompton, Richmal. *Just William*. Macmillan, 2010.
Cusk, Rachel. *Kudos*. Faber & Faber, 2019.
Dahl, Roald. *Fantastic Mr Fox*. Knopf, 1970.
Dann, Colin. *The Animals of Farthing Wood*. Egmont, 2016.
Daum, Meghan. 'The Dog Exception'. *Unspeakable: and Other Subjects of Discussion*. Farrar, Straus and Giroux, 2014.
De Bernières, Louis. *Red Dog*. Pantheon, 2001.
Defoe, Daniel. *Robinson Crusoe*. C. H. Clarke, 1856.
DiCamillo, Kate. *Because of Winn-Dixie*. Walker Books, 2000.
Dick, Philip K. 'Roog'. *The Collected Stories of Philip K. Dick Vol 1*. Gollancz, 2023.
Dickens, Charles. *Dombey and Son*. Bradbury & Evans, 1848.
Dickens, Charles. Letter to W. H. Wills, 9 December 1951. *The Letters of Charles Dickens, vol. 1. 1833–1856*. Edited by Mamie Dickens and Georgina Hogarth. projectgutenberg.org
Dickens, Charles. *Oliver Twist*. Penguin, 2003.
Dickens, Charles. *The Letters of Charles Dickens*. Edited by Georgina Hogarth and Mamie Dickens. Chapman & Hall, 1880.

Dickens, Charles. *The Uncommercial Traveller*. Everyman, 1911.
Dostoevsky, Fyodor. *The Idiot*. Translated by Constance Garnett. Dell Publishing, 1962.
du Maurier, Daphne. *Rebecca*. Doubleday, 1938.
Dumas, Alexandre. *Mary Stuart Queen of Scots*. Merriam Company Publishers, 1896.
Dumas, Alexandre. *The Count of Monte Cristo*. Tor, 1998.
Dunmore, Helen. *Birdcage Walk*. Atlantic, 2017.
Durrell, Gerald. *My Family and Other Animals*. Penguin, 2000.
Eliot, George. *Adam Bede*. Oxford University Press, 1998.
Eliot, George. *Middlemarch*. Norton, 1977.
Eliot, T. S. *Old Possum's Book of Practical Cats*. Faber & Faber, 1962.
Emanuel, Walter. *A Dog Day*. E. P. Dutton, 1919.
Emily Dickinson Museum. 'Carlo (1849–1866), dog'. emilydickinsonmuseum.org
Emshwiller, Carol. *Carmen Dog*. Peapod Classics, 2004.
Englert, J. F. *A Dog About Town*. Bantam Dell, 2007.
Ephron, Nora. *I Feel Bad About My Neck*. Doubleday, 2020.
Estés, Clarissa Pinkola. *Women Who Run With the Wolves*. Ballantine, 1995.
Estes, Eleanor. *Ginger Pye*. Harcourt Brace, 1979.
Faulkner, William. 'The Bear'. *Go Down, Moses*. Curtis, 1942.
Ferrante, Elena. T*he Days of Abandonment*. Europa, 2021.
Fielding, Helen. Bridget Jones: *The Edge of Reason*. Penguin, 2004.
Fitzgerald, F. Scott. *The Great Gatsby*. Penguin, 1950.
Flaubert, Gustave. *Madame Bovary*. Penguin, 2001.
Fleming, Abraham. 'A straunge and terrible wunder wrought very late in the parish church of Bongay, a tovvn of no great distance from the citie of Norwich, namely the fourth of this August, in ye yeere of our Lord 1577 in a great tempest of violent raine, lightning, and thunder, the like wherof hath been seldome seene. With the appeerance of an horrible shaped thing, sensibly perceiued of the people then and there assembled. Drawen into a plain method according to the written copye. By Abraham Fleming.' In the digital collection Early English Books Online. https://name.umdl.umich.edu/A00943.0001.001. University of Michigan Library Digital Collections.
Fletcher, C. A. *A Boy and His Dog at the End of the World*. Orbit, 2019.
Franzen, Jonathan. *Purity*. Picador, 2015.
Fuller, Claire. *Unsettled Ground*. Fig Tree, 2021.
Gaarder, Jostein. *Sophie's World*. Wiedenfeld & Nicolson, 2015.
Galbaldon, Diana. *Drums of Autumn*. Delacorte Press, 1997.
Galsworthy, John. *Memories*. Heinemann, 1920.
García Márquez, Gabriel. 'Eyes of a Blue Dog'. Translated by Gregory Rabassa. The New Yorker, 1 May 1978.
Gardner, Erle Stanley. *The Case of the Howling Dog*. Ankerwycke , 2015.
Garmus, Bonnie. *Lessons in Chemistry*. Penguin, 2023.
Garner, Helen. *How to End a Story: Collected Diaries*. Orion, 2025.
Gaskell, Elizabeth. *The Poor Clare*. Melville House, 2013.
Gispon, Fred. *Old Yeller*. Harper, 1956.
Godden, Rumer. *Black Narcissus*. Albatross, 1947.
Gogol, Nikolai. *The Government Inspector. Gogol: Plays and Selected Writings*. Northwestern University Press, 1994.
Graham, Winston. *Ross Poldark*. Pan, 2015.
Green, Ward. 'Happy Dan the Cynical Dog'. *Cosmopolitan*, February 1945.
Greene, Graham. *The Human Factor*. Simon & Schuster, 1978.
Grimm, Jacob, and Grimm, Wilhelm. *Grimms' Fairy Tales*. Wordsworth, 1993.

Grogan, John. *Marley and Me*. Hodder & Stoughton, 2008.

Haddon, Mark. *The Curious Incident of the Dog in the Night-Time*. Doubleday, 2003.

Haig, Matt. *How to Stop Time*. Canongate, 2017.

Hall, Sarah. *The Wolf Border*. Faber & Faber, 2015.

Hammett, Dashiell. *The Thin Man*. Penguin, 2012.

Hardy, Thomas. *Far From the Madding Crowd*. Harper & Brothers, 1918.

Hawthorne, Nathaniel. *The Complete Writings of Nathaniel Hawthorne: Passages from the American Note-Books*. Houghton, Mifflin & Company, 1868.

Heaney, Seamus. 'A Dog Was Crying To-night in Wicklow Also'. *Opened Ground: Poems 1966–1996*. Faber and Faber, 1998.

Heaney, Seamus. 'Kinship'. *North*. Oxford University Press, 1976.

Heisey, Monica. *Really Good, Actually*. Fourth Estate, 2023.

Hempel, Amy. *The Dog of the Marriage*. Quercus, 2009.

Henry, O. 'Memoirs of a Yellow Dog'. *The Four Million*. Doubleday, 1906.

Herbert, James. *Fluke*. New English Library, 1977.

Herriot, James. *Only One Woof*. St Martin's Press, 1985.

Heyer, Georgette. *Frederica*. Bodley Head, 1965.

Hill, Susan. *The Woman in Black*. Vintage, 2012.

Hodgson, William Hope. *The House on the Borderland*. Penguin, 2024.

Hoffmann, E. T. A. *The Nutcracker and the Mouse King*. D. Appleton & Co., 1853.

Homer, *The Odyssey*. Trans. Robert Fitzgerald. Doubleday, 1961.

Honeyman, Gail. *Eleanor Oliphant is Completely Fine*. Thorndike, 2017.

Housman, Clemence. *The Were-Wolf*. Arno, 1976.

Hughes, Ted. 'Roger the Dog'. *Collected Animal Poems Vol 1–4*. Faber & Faber, 1995.

Hughes, Ted. 'The Thought-Fox'. *The Hawk in the Rain*. Harper, 1957.

Hugo, Victor. *Les Misérables*. Penguin, 2015.

Ingalls Wilder, Laura. *Little House on the Prairie*. Arcturus, 1956.

Irving, Washington. *Rip Van Winkle*. Lippincott, 1967.

Jackson, Shirley. T*he Haunting of Hill House*. Chivers, 2011.

James, Henry. *Selected Letters*. Edited by Leon Edel. Belknap Press, 1987.

Jansson, Tove. *Moominland Midwinter*. Avon, 1976.

Jerome, Jerome K. *Three Men in a Boat*. Simpkin, Marshall & Co., 1889.

Joyce, James. *Ulysses*. Pitman Press, 1952.

Juster, Norton. *The Phantom Tollbooth*. Random House, 2000.

Kafka, Franz. 'Investigations of a Dog'. *Selected Short Stories of Franz Kafka*. Modern Library, 1952.

King-Smith, Dick. *The Sheep-Pig*. Puffin, 2017.

King, Stephen. *Cujo*. Warner, 1992.

King, Stephen. *Fairy Tale*. Hodder & Stoughton, 2022.

King, Stephen. *The Stand*. Doubleday, 1978.

Kingfisher, T. *The Twisted Ones*. Titan, 2020.

Kingsolver, Barbara. *Animal Dreams*. Harper Collins, 1990.

Kipling, Rudyard. 'Four-Feet'. *Collected Dog Stories*. Macmillan, 1940.

Kipling, Rudyard. *The Jungle Book*. Oxford University Press, 2008.

Kipling, Rudyard. *Thy Servant a Dog: Told by Boots*. Macmillan, 1931.

Kjelgaard, Jim. *Big Red*. Holiday House, 1945.

Knight, Eric. *Lassie Come-Home*. Cassell, 1942.

Koontz, Dean. *Watchers*. Headline, 1987.

Kundera, Milan. *The Unbearable Lightness of Being*. Faber & Faber, 1984.

Lamott, Anne. *Bird by Bird: Some Instructions on Writing and Life*. Pantheon, 1994.

Lawrence, D. H. 'Bibbles'. *The Complete Poems of D. H. Lawrence.* Penguin, 1989.
Lawrence, D. H. *Lady Chatterley's Lover.* Guild Publishing, 1981.
Le Guin, Ursula K. 'Dogs, cats and dancers – thoughts about beauty'. *The Wave in the Mind: Talks and Essays on the Writer, the Reader and the Imagination.* Shambhala 2004.
Lear, Edward. *A Book of Nonsense.* James Miller, 1863.
Lewis, C. S. *The Lion, the Witch and the Wardrobe.* Harper Collins, 2008.
Lispector, Clarice. *A Breath of Life (Pulsations).* Translated by Johnny Lorenz. New Directions, 2012.
Lockwood, Patricia. *No One is Talking About This.* Bloomsbury, 2021.
Lofting, Hugh. *The Story of Dr Dolittle.* Frederick A. Stokes, 1920.
London, Jack. *To Build a Fire and Other Stories.* Reader's Digest, 1994.
London, Jack. *White Fang and The Call of the Wild.* Penguin, 1903.
London, Jack. *White Fang.* Outing Publishing, 1906.
Mann, Thomas. *Doctor Faustus.* Translated by H. T. Lowe-Porter. Oxford University Press, 1959.
Mannix, Daniel P. *The Fox and the Hound.* Dutton, 1967.
Mansfield, Katherine. 'A Man and His Dog'. *The Dove's Nest and Other Stories.* Constable & Company, 1923.
Martin, George R. R. *A Game of Thrones.* Bantam Books, 2016.
Marx, Karl. Quoted in: Padover, Saul Kussiel. *Karl Marx: An Intimate Biography.* McGraw-Hill, 1978.
Matheson, Richard. *I Am Legend / Hell House.* Quality Paperback Book Club, 2006.
Maxwell, Gavin. *Ring of Bright Water.* Folio Society, 1960.
Maxwell, William. *So Long, See You Tomorrow.* Ballantine Books, 1981.
McCarthy, Cormac. *The Crossing.* Vintage, 1995.
Melville, Herman. *Redburn: His First Voyage at Sea.* Harper & Brothers, 1849.
Montgomery, L. M. *Rilla of Ingleside.* Frederic A. Stokes, 1921.
Morante, Elsa. *History.* Translated by William Weaver. Steerforth Press, 2000.
Morpurgo, Michael. *Little Foxes.* Mammoth, 1990.
Morrey, Beth. *Saving Missy.* Harper Collins, 2020.
Morris, Willie. *My Dog Skip.* Random House, 1995.
Murakami, Haruki. *Sputnik Sweetheart.* Knopf, 2001.
Murdoch, Iris. *The Green Knight.* Penguin, 1995.
Murdoch, Iris. *The Philosopher's Pupil.* Viking, 1983.
Myerson, Julie. *The Stopped Heart.* Vintage, 2017.
Nabokov, Vladimir. *Pnin.* Vintage, 1989.
Naylor, Phyllis Reynolds. *Shiloh.* Aladdin, 2000.
Ness, Patrick. *The Knife of Never Letting Go.* Walker, 2009.
Nin, Anaïs. *A Café in Space: The Anaïs Nin Literary Journal. Volume 5,* 2008. Edited by Paul Herron. Sky Blue Press, 2011.
Nix, Garth. *Lirael.* Harper Collins, 2003.
Nunez, Sigrid. *The Friend.* Riverhead Books, 2019.
O'Hagan, Andrew. *The Life and Opinions of Maf the Dog, and of His Friend Marilyn Monroe.* Faber & Faber, 2010.
Oliver, Mary. *Dog Songs.* Thorndike Press, 2014.
Orwell, George. 'A Hanging'. *George Orwell: Essays.* Penguin, 2000.
Orwell, George. *Animal Farm.* ELBS, 1965.
Ouida. *A Dog of Flanders, The Nürnberg Stove, and Other Stories.* Lippincott, 1909.
Palacio, R. J. *Wonder.* Doubleday, 2012.
Parker, Dorothy. 'Verse for a Certain Dog'. *Enough Rope.* Boni & Liveright, 1926.

Parker, Matthew. *Goldeneye: Where Bond Was Born: Ian Fleming's Jamaica*. Hutchinson, 2014.
Parker, Robert B. *Pastime*. Putnam, 1991.
Paterson, Katherine. *The Bridge to Terabithia*. Trumpet Club, 1987.
Paver, Michelle. *Thin Air*. Orion, 2016.
Perkins Gilman, Charlotte. *Herland*. Hesperus, 2015.
Pliny the Elder. *Natural History: A Selection*. Penguin, 1991.
Poe, Edgar Allan. 'The Business Man'. *The Complete Edgar Allan Poe: Tales*. Chatham River Press, 1981.
Poe, Edgar Allan. *The Fall of the House of Usher & Other Tales*. New American Library, 1960.
Pope, Alexander. 'On the collar of a dog presented by Mr Pope to the Prince of Wales'. In: Graves, Richard. *The Festoon: A Collection of Epigrams, Ancient and Modern*. Robinson and Roberts, 1766.
Pope, Alexander. *The Rape of the Lock*. Bedford Books, 1998.
Potter, Beatrix. *The Tale of Ginger & Pickles*. F. Warne, 1909.
Pratchett, Terry. *Men at Arms*. HarperPrism, 1997.
Pratchett, Terry. *Moving Pictures*. Harper, 2008.
Pullman, Philip. *His Dark Materials: Omnibus*. Scholastic, 2000.
Pynchon, Thomas. *Against the Day*. Penguin, 2007.
Crafton, Luke. Quoted in: Antiques Roadshow. pbs.org, 28 January 2019.
Rawls, Wilson. *Where the Red Fern Grows*. Bantam Doubleday Dell, 1996.
Repplier, Agnes. *In the Dozy Hours and Other Papers*. Houghton, Mifflin & Co. 1894.
Rooney, Sally. *Intermezzo*. Faber & Faber, 2024.
Rowley, Stephen. *Lily and the Octopus*. Simon & Schuster, 2016.
Rushdie, Salman. *Luka and the Fire of Life*. Jonathan Cape, 2010.
Sackville-West, Vita. *Faces: Profiles of Dogs*. Harvill Press, 1961.
Safran Foer, Jonathan. *Everything is Illuminated*. Penguin, 2003.
Saint-Exupéry, Antoine de. *The Little Prince*. Thorndike Press, 2005.
Salinger, J. D. *The Catcher in the Rye*. Little, Brown, 1951.
Sayers, Dorothy L. *Gaudy Night*. Avon Books, 1968.
Sayers, Dorothy L. *Whose Body?* Avon, 1923.
Sebold, Alice. *The Lovely Bones*. Picador, 2003.
Shakespeare, William. *A Midsummer Night's Dream*. Longman, 2000.
Shakespeare, William. *Julius Caesar*, Act 3, Scene 1. Oxford University Press, 1992.
Shakespeare, William. *King Lear*. Act 3, Scene 6. Macmillan, 2009.
Shakespeare, William. *The Taming of the Shrew*. Act 1, Scene 1. Oxford University Press, 2001.
Shakespeare, William. *The Two Gentlemen of Verona*. Dover Publications, 2015.
Shelley, Mary. *Frankenstein*. Everyman, 1994.
Shorter, Clement King. *The Brontës: Life and Letters*. Hodder and Stoughton, 1908.
Simak, Clifford. *City*. Ace Books, 1976.
Simmons, Ernest J. *Chekhov: A Biography*. Little, Brown, 1962.
Smith, Dodie. *The Hundred and One Dalmatians*. Penguin, 1957.
Smith, Zadie. 'A Woman with a Little Dog'. *Intimations*. Penguin, 2020.
Smith, Zadie. 'Crazy They Call Me'. *The New Yorker*. 26 February 2017.
Spencer, William Robert. 'Beth Gelert, Or The Grave of a Greyhound'. allpoetry.com.
Stapledon, Olaf. *Odd John & Sirius: Two Science-fiction Novels*. Dover, 1972.
Stein, Garth. *The Art of Racing in the Rain*. Harper Collins, 2008.
Stein, Gertrude. *Geography and Plays*. Four Seas Company, 1922.

Stein, Gertrude. Letter to Alexander Woollcott, December 1935. *The Letters of Gertrude Stein and Thornton Wilder*. Edited by Edward M. Burns and Ulla E. Dydo with William Rice. Yale University Press, 1996.
Steinbeck, John. Quoted in: Creamer, Ella. 'Of Mice and Men first-draft fragment torn up by Steinbeck's dog goes to auction'. *Guardian*, 29 September 2023.
Steinbeck, John. *Travels with Charley*. Heinemann, 1916.
Stoker, Bram. Dracula. Random House, 1897.
Styron, William. 'Walking with Aquinnah'. *Havanas in Camelot*. Random House, 2008.
Swift, Jonathan. *Gulliver's Travels*. Norton, 1961.
Tartt, Donna. *The Goldfinch*. Little, Brown, 2013.
Tartt, Donna. *The Secret History*. Penguin, 1993.
Thackeray, William Makepeace. *Vanity Fair*. Smith, Elder & Co, 1868.
Thomas, Dylan. 'The Song of the Mischievous Dog'. *The Poems of Dylan Thomas*. New Directions, 1971.
Tokarczuk, Olga. *Drive Your Plow Over the Bones of the Dead*. Fitzcarraldo, 2018.
Tolkien, J. R. R. 'Roverandom'. *Tales from the Perilous Realm*. Houghton Mifflin Harcourt, 2008.
Tolkien, J. R. R. *Farmer Giles of Ham*. In: *Poems and Stories*. Houghton Mifflin, 1994.
Tolkien, J. R. R. *The Silmarillion*. Edited by Christopher Tolkien. Harper Collins, 2011.
Tolkien, J. R. R. *The Fellowship of the Ring*. Ballantine Books, 1973.
Tolstoy, Leo. 'Búlka'. *The Complete Works of Count Tolstoy, Vol XII*. Translated by Leo Wiener. Dana Estes & Company, 1904.
Tolstoy, Leo. *Anna Karenina*. Translated by Louise and Aylmer Maude. Vintage, 2010.
Tomasi de Lampedusa, Giuseppe. *The Leopard*. Translated by Archibald Colquhoun. Reprint Society, 1961.
Townsend, Sue. *The Adrian Mole Diaries*. Methuen, 1985.
Trollope, Anthony. 'The Spotted Dog'. The Spotted Dog & Other Stories. Alan Sutton Publishing, 1983.
Twain, Mark. 'A Dog's Tale'. Project Gutenberg, 2006. https://www.gutenberg.org/files/3174/3174-h/3174-h.htm
Twain, Mark. *Autobiography of Mark Twain Vol. 3*. University of California Press, 2009.
Twain, Mark. Letter to William D. Howells, 2 April 1899. *Selected Mark Twain–Howells Letters, 1872–1910*. Bellknap Press, 1967.
Updike, John. 'Another Dog's Death'. *Collected Poems, 1953–1993*. Knopf, 1993.
Updike, John. *The Witches of Eastwick*. Deutsch, 1984.
Van Dine, S. S. *The Kennel Murder Case*. Scribner, 1984.
Verne, Jules. *Dick Sand, A Captain at Fifteen*. G. Munro, 1878.
Vonnegut, Kurt. *The Sirens of Titan*. Delacorte Press, 1959.
Walker, Alice. 'Crimes against dog'. In *Dog is my Co-Pilot: Great Writers on the World's Oldest Friendship*. Crown, 2003.
Waters, Sarah. *The Little Stranger*. Virago, 2009.
Waugh, Evelyn. *Brideshead Revisited*. Penguin, 1922.
Waugh, Evelyn. *The Loved One*. Vintage, 1948.
Wells, H. G. *The Invisible Man*. Fontana, 1959.
Wharton, Edith. Diary titled *Quaderno dello Studente*. Quoted in: Smith, John W. 'From the Director' *Archives of American Art Journal*, vol. 48, no. 3/4, 2009.
Wharton, Edith. Letter to Charles Eliot Norton, June 1908. Quoted in: 'Dogs at the Mount'. The Mount: Edith Wharton's Home. edithwharton.org.
Wharton, Edith. Letter to William R. Tyler, 16 May 1937. *The Letters of Edith Wharton*. Edited by R. W. B. Lewis and Nancy Lewis. Scribner, 1988.

White, E. B. 'Two Letters, Both Open'. *The New Yorker*. 14 April 1951.
White, E. B. *Essays of E. B. White*. Harper & Row, 1977.
White, T. H. Quoted in: Townsend Warner, Sylvia. *T. H. White: A Biography*. Viking, 1968.
Wilkie, Collins. *My Lady's Money*. In: *The Haunted Hotel: A Mystery of Modern Venice; to which is added My Lady's Money*. Chatto & Windus, 1892.
Willis, Connie. *To Say Nothing of the Dog*. Bantam, 1997.
Winterson, Jeanette. 'The Twenty-four Hour Dog'. *The World and Other Places*. Jonathan Cape, 1998.
Wodehouse, P. G. *Author! Author!* Simon & Schuster, 1962.
Wodehouse, P.G. *Tales from the Drones Club*. IPL, 1991.
Wood, Charlotte. *The Weekend*. Sceptre, 2020.
Woolf, Virginia. *A Writer's Diary*. Harvest, 1954.
Woolf, Virginia. *Flush: A Biography*. Harcourt, Brace and Company, 1933.
Woolf, Virginia. *Mrs Dalloway*. Penguin, 1992.
Wordsworth, William. 'Tribute to the Memory of the Same Dog'. https://allpoetry.com/Tribute-To-The-Memory-Of-The-Same-Dog
Wroblewski, David. *The Story of Edgar Sawtelle*. Bond Street, 2008.
Wynne Jones, Diana. *Dogsbody*. Methuen, 1988.
Yoder, Rachel. *Nightbitch*. Vintage, 2021.
Zelazny, Roger. *A Night in the Lonesome October*. William Morrow & Co, 1993.

Dear Reader,

We'd love your attention for one more page to tell you about the crisis in children's reading, and what we can all do.

Studies have shown that reading for fun is the **single biggest predictor of a child's future life chances** – more than family circumstance, parents' educational background or income. It improves academic results, mental health, wealth, communication skills, ambition and happiness.[1]

The number of children reading for fun is in rapid decline. Young people have a lot of competition for their time. In 2024, 1 in 10 children and young people in the UK aged 5 to 18 did not own a single book at home.[2]

Hachette works extensively with schools, libraries and literacy charities, but here are some ways we can all raise more readers:

- Reading to children for just 10 minutes a day makes a difference
- Don't give up if children aren't regular readers – there will be books for them!
- Visit bookshops and libraries to get recommendations
- Encourage them to listen to audiobooks
- Support school libraries
- Give books as gifts

There's a lot more information about how to encourage children to read on our website: **www.RaisingReaders.co.uk**

Thank you for reading.

---

[1] OECD, '21st-Century Readers: Developing Literacy Skills in a Digital World', 2021, https://www.oecd.org/en/publications/21st-century-readers_a83d84cb-en.html

[2] National Literacy Trust, 'Book Ownership in 2024'. November 2024, https://literacytrust.org.uk/research-services/research-reports/book-ownership-in-2024